First-Time Valentine
MARY J FORBES

D1513509

⊗™ MILLS & BOON®
Pure reading pleasure™

First published in Great Britain 2009
by Harlequin Mills & Boon Limited,
Eton House, 18-24 Paradise Road, Richmond, Surrey TW9 1SR

© Harlequin Books S.A. 2008

Special thanks and acknowledgement are given to Mary J Forbes for
her contribution to The Wilder Family mini-series.

ISBN: 978 0 263 87022 0

23-0209

Harlequin Mills & Boon policy is to use papers that are
natural, renewable and recyclable products and made from
wood grown in sustainable forests. The logging and
manufacturing processes conform to the legal environmental
regulations of the country of origin.

Printed and bound in Spain
by Litografia Rosés S.A., Barcelona

"Ella, can I see you?"

She pretended to misunderstand. "I need to finish my rounds."

"I meant after. Once I've left the hospital. I'll be staying in Walnut River for a couple weeks."

"Oh? So you *do* have family here?" Would he admit it now?

"Trying to get me off track, Doc? I'm asking if you'll have dinner with me once I'm discharged."

She shook her head. "It's just that you're very predictable. It makes me wonder how many other nurses and doctors you've wooed."

He didn't blink. "Not a one."

She huffed a laugh. "I'll bet not for lack of trying."

"Don't have to try, Doc."

"Ah. Women drop like flies at your feet, then?"

A wicked grin. "Something like that."

"Good to know." She lifted her chin. "Well, Mr Sumner, don't let me get in their way."

Available in February 2009
from Mills & Boon®
Special Edition

MARY J FORBES

grew up on a farm amid horses, cattle, crisp
hay and broad blue skies. As a child, she drew
and wrote of her surroundings and in primary
school composed her first story about a little
lame pony. Years later, she worked as an
accountant, then as a reporter-photographer
for a small-town newspaper, before attaining
an honours degree in education to become a
teacher. She has also written and published
short fiction stories.

A romantic by nature, Mary loves walking along
the ocean shoreline, sitting by the fire on snowy
or rainy evenings and two-stepping around
the dance floor to a good country song – all
with her own real-life hero, of course. Mary
would love to hear from her readers at www.
maryjforbes.com.

Chapter One

J.D. opened his eyes to a murky dawn.

For a moment, he was at a loss with his surroundings. Oh, yeah. Back in Walnut River, Massachusetts, his hometown—and the hospital of his birth.

He groaned as memories of a long night of pain and fitful dreams rushed together. He lay in a hospital bed. IV attached to his vein. His right knee…

He did not want to consider the mess there.

Outside his room, the hospital woke. In his head, memories tumbled. The board meeting last night. The snowstorm. His knee popping like a firecracker as he slipped on those damned icy steps. And then…*oh, man*…the killing pain.

Had he blacked out? He couldn't remember. Just the crazy pain.

He should've had his knee fixed years ago. Hadn't he learned back in high school playing basketball? When the doctor told him about "jumper's knee"? Had he taken the man's advice? No. Instead, he'd ignored every recommendation and for years depended on over-the-counter painkillers. And then he'd defied fate seven years ago by joining the Northeastern HealthCare basketball team when the company hired his ambitious mind.

Arrogant jackass is what you were.

J.D. grunted. Damn this February weather. Damn the ice and snow, and why he'd returned yesterday to this armpit dot on the Massachusetts map. And damn the fact that he was now doomed to wait for surgery by the esteemed Dr. Ella Wilder, another one of the family of Wilders he'd come to lock horns with—well, not lock horns, to wine and dine and sway to realize that NHC's contemporary model of practicing medicine was the way of the future. A model second-to-none in efficiency. A model favoring corporate-run medicine, not the old-fashioned methods prevalent in this quaint little hospital.

If he did his job right, Walnut River General would be brought under NHC's generous umbrella in a matter of months, a move that would benefit patients and doctors with some modernity—with a capital *M*.

But first he needed to get out of here. Fast.

Six hours later and still waiting for his surgery, he realized fast was not a key part of this hospital's policy and his apprehension had mushroomed into full-blown anxiety. Okay, they'd told him the E.R. was having a chaotic day. But he hadn't seen the doctor—any doctor—since he'd been there.

Stop worrying, J.D. Your gurney is third in line for the O.R. Won't be long now. Which did not calm him at all.

Goddammit. Didn't they know he hated Walnut River General? His mother—Grace Sumner—had died here. Died of a blood clot in her brain—as a result of the C-section at his birth, or so Pops maintained.

You go to the hospital to die. End of story. As far back as J.D. remembered the old man's words had been a slogan in their house.

Yes, Grace was the reason J.D. had avoided getting his knee repaired years ago. Nobody was cutting into him, causing blood clots. Last night, however, he knew he could no longer dodge surgery. It was either that or end up walking with a cane for the rest of his life, *plus* attracting arthritis before he was forty.

So, where was the female Wilder? He hated to admit it, but the way she touched him, spoke, smiled last night in the E.R....

"Mr. Sumner," she had said upon entering his curtained cubicle. "I'm Dr. Ella Wilder. I hear you fell on some steps and banged up your knee." Against the collar of her white lab coat hung a hot-pink stethoscope.

"Should sue the hospital," he'd ground out, gazing at her through half-closed eyes. He hadn't expected a woman doctor. Nor one resembling a French fashion model.

"Suing won't heal your knee, sir," she informed him, dipping her head to examine his exposed leg.

The paramedic—Mike O'Rourke was it?—had found J.D. sprawled across the snowy steps by the hospital parking lot. In the E.R., the man had cut away the expensive cloth from his right pant leg, easier for radiology to take X-rays.

Ella Wilder snapped on a pair of surgical gloves and tested the wounded area gently. "Tell me when it hurts."

He winced; she nodded. "I'm sending you for an MRI."

"Think I broke something?" He tried to lift up on his elbows.

"According to the X-rays, no. However, I'd like more information about the soft tissues around and under your kneecap. We'll also do some blood work to see if there's a sign of arthritis."

"Arthritis?" He bit his bottom lip as she gently probed the distended knee. "You saying—" a pained grunt "—I'm getting *old*?"

"Not at all." The dark bob of her hair swung along the line of her jaw as she removed the gloves. "Arthritis can happen at any age."

"Terrific. Worst-case scenario?"

"Let's see what the MRI brings. If it's what I suspect, we'll do surgery tomorrow once the swelling subsides." She offered a smile and it blew through his pain like a breeze on the Cayman coast. "Meantime, we'll keep you off your feet tonight and get some pills into you."

"Don't need pills," he mumbled. "Don't wanna stay here."

She patted his hand. "Trust me, the pills will help

while we wait for the injury to settle and the throbbing to lessen."

In spite of his pain, a corner of his mouth lifted. "You going to be my doctor?"

"If your injury is what I suspect, then yes, I will be."

His eyes closed. "Good. I like the idea of throbbing for you."

God almighty. Were you delusional last night, J.D., or just a total jerk? He couldn't believe he'd actually uttered those words. To a doctor, no less. He owed her an apology, preferably before the operation. The last thing he needed was for her to cut into him with payback on her mind.

Across the O.R.'s inpatient waiting bay, an old guy hacked as if his lungs were full of gravel. From out of nowhere a nurse hurried to raise the guy's head, asking how he was holding out, and if anyone sat with his wife and did his son still work at the paper? J.D. groaned. The old home-week chitchat he could do without.

He checked the wall clock. 12:23 p.m. Eighteen hours since he'd tumbled down those steps that led to the parking lot across the hospital's entrance lane.

Never in his life had he been this idle. Okay, admittedly the care so far had been excellent. Nurses, doctors and technicians were gentle and promptly got him whatever he asked for: magazines, water, juice…everything except an early surgery slot.

New York, that's where he should be, in his plush office with its cherrywood desk and his proficient secretary. Hell, he hadn't scratched and clawed his way to the rung of executive for Northeastern HealthCare by stopping to smell the Mayflowers.

He grunted. He'd be hard-pressed to find any flower in the concrete jungle where he worked.

"Hello, Mr. Sumner," a soft female voice said before blue scrubs and *her* face came into view.

God, she was one appealing woman. And those dark eyes… A brown he couldn't quite describe—until he thought of the fancy bag of hazelnuts his secretary had bought him last Christmas.

"How are you feeling?" Ella Wilder asked, unaware of where his thoughts traveled. This afternoon the bell of her pink stethoscope was tucked into a breast pocket.

"Bored as hell," he grumbled.

She offered a quick smile. "Won't be much longer. I have one surgery ahead of you which will take about thirty minutes." Moving down to his iced knee, she marked the spot where she would do her work. "The swelling has decreased. That's good."

Her hair, he saw now, was a study of browns and blacks. Today she'd clipped the thick locks behind her ears.

She asked several more questions about his injury, ensured he was Jared Devlin Sumner, and had he taken his meds?

"I gave all that info to the nurse," he said, annoyed as hell that through everything he couldn't stop taking inventory of her body.

"We like to double check. It's standard procedure." She jotted a few extra notes on his chart. "Do you have family here, Mr. Sumner?"

"No." Well, he did, but his old man was no one's business. "This isn't a big deal, is it?" He would never admit it, but the notion of having his flesh divided by a knife scared him witless.

Her expressive eyes held his. "Everything should go fine."

"Should? Not sure I like the sound of that." He tried to swallow past the fist in his throat.

Again the smile. He liked her mouth. The cute little body, the shape of her eyes…that great mouth…. Hell, he liked everything he saw.

"You'll be fine, Mr. Sumner."

"Maybe I'll take legal action. Those stairs should've been de-iced." All right, he sounded like one of his dad's scratched records, constantly playing the same line over again.

One dark brow curved. "Were you wearing snow boots?"

"I had proper footwear."

The brow remained high. "Not from what I saw last night."

When he was wearing his five hundred dollar pair of Gucci loafers. "Fine. You've made your point," he grouched.

She patted his hand. "You wouldn't be the first to misjudge our weather."

"I grew up here." Now why mention that?

This time both eyebrows sprang. "Oh?"

"Long time ago."

"And no doubt well before my time."

He grinned. "I'm not much older than you, Doc."

Going with the years in med school, he estimated she was in her early thirties.

"According to your chart you're seven years older." Her cheeks flushed and she looked away. "See you in the O.R."

"Hold on—you're twenty-nine? Are you a real doctor?"

Her nostrils flared. "I finished my residency last year."

"Should I trust you with my knee?" The flip tone contained his thread of worry, he knew.

"You can trust me."

"Where have I heard that before?"

"I'll see you in surgery, Mr. Sumner." She walked away, tidy in her blue scrubs—determination in her eyes.

J.D. swallowed. He'd offended her twice in less than twenty-four hours and he was going under the knife. *Her* knife.

And he'd forgotten to apologize.

Should I trust you with my knee? The words plagued Ella's mind as she scrubbed in for his surgery.

Lord, she thought, *if he only knew how close his question struck.* Well, she wouldn't think of it. She would not. Instead, she inhaled slowly and checked the equipment tray readied by the scrub nurse. *Interning is behind you. You're a doctor now. With excellent surgical talent. You know what to do.*

Her counselor's mantra, calming her pounding heart and the jitters edging into her fingers. *One more deep breath....*

They wheeled Sumner in and she saw he was calm and slightly drowsy from the sedative administered twenty minutes before.

Shelly, the circulating nurse, went through the preoperative checklist again, ensuring he was the correct patient via his armband, X-rays, consent forms, lab results. Next Brad, Ella's anesthesiologist, explained his role to her patient.

The pain will be gone soon, she told him mentally. On the monitor, she scanned Sumner's vitals.

"Good to go," Brad informed her. Patient was out.

"Let's get started then."

An hour later, Ella pulled off her soiled surgical gloves and tossed them in the disposable bin. She had repaired his damaged cartilage. He'd been lucky—the kneecap hadn't shifted, and while the soft tissue had bruised, it hadn't sustained severe injury. However, the fall had wreaked havoc on his right meniscus—torn the cartilage from its mooring—and after studying the X-rays last night and the MRI this morning, Ella had known J.D.'s repair would entail the arthroscopic surgery she had just performed.

Now he was on his way to recovery. She'd check on him in fifteen minutes, but first she needed a drink of water. Surgeries with their intense lights and stress always dehydrated her. In the small doctor's lounge down the hall she found her internist brother, Peter, sitting at one of the two small tables reading several pages of a letter, a coffee at his right hand.

"Hey, Peter." Ella reached into the fridge for the liter of Evian she'd brought that morning from home.

He gave her a glance. "El."

She sat across from him, stretched her legs, took a long pull on the water and jutted her chin at the pages. "What's up?"

"More crap from the state medical board. They're claiming we're unethical in our methods, that we're focusing too much on coddling—their word—patients and not enough on speed of recovery and effectiveness of treatment." He gathered the pages into the big brown folder marked Dr. P. Wilder, Chief of Staff. The word *confidential* had been typed above his name.

"Should you be telling me this?" she asked, hoping he would say no. She had no time or interest in crazy allegations, especially when they alluded to a political agenda. Having already heard the rumors and innuendos, she simply tried to focus on her work.

Undoubtedly some of those rumors had evolved from the tug-of-war between Peter and his fiancée, Bethany Holloway—before they'd fallen in love. As a newcomer to Walnut River and the hospital board, Bethany had initially advocated Northeastern HealthCare's takeover of Walnut River General. Until Peter convinced her NHC's financial "support" would disintegrate the heart of the hospital.

Now, he shrugged his big shoulders. "You know the most of it already," he said.

"I don't want to," Ella said honestly. "I was never any good at political science."

He gave her a smile. "Aw, El. You were the brains of the family. We all knew that the minute you turned two and told Mom she'd made an extra cookie for Anna."

Their sister who had estranged herself from the family almost ten years ago. Ella rubbed her forehead. "I wish…"

"What?"

"That Anna believed in our love."

"She's got to work it out herself, Ella."

Momentarily they remained silent, the hospital's sounds drifting through the open door: a medicine cart's squeaky wheels in the hallway, the beep of someone's pager, the jingle of a maintenance staffer's keys. Sounds that had soothed Ella since she'd first toddled down the wide, polished corridors with her daddy, Dr. James Wilder.

Oh! Sometimes missing him would hit her so hard she had to catch her breath.

She thought of the man whose knee she'd repaired. Of course she'd recognized him last night. J. D. Sumner, executive of Northeastern HealthCare had arrived two days ago from New York City to woo the hospital board. A man with an agenda that, according to Peter, would uproot her father's legacy and the principles of Walnut River General.

A man who had the greenest eyes—like moss on a forest tree....

Moss on a tree? Sheesh, Ella. Have you lost it?

Shoving the silly analogy aside, she said, "Sumner's surgery went well, although he'll be using crutches for a few days." Her lips twitched. "I wouldn't put it past him to show up in the boardroom with his butt hanging out of a hospital gown."

Peter flashed a grin. "I'll tell Beth. She's doing some digging on who's feeding the wolves." He tapped the folder.

"Speaking of which, I need to check the one in my recovery."

With a last gulp of water, she deposited the empty bottle into the recycle bin and headed down the hallway.

She still couldn't believe she'd given Sumner that tidbit about her age and experience. Thank goodness, she hadn't blurted out anything else—such as *I have confidence issues in the O.R. and am seeing a psychologist in Springfield.*

God forbid.

Walking into recovery, she saw that consciousness wove through her patient's mind, a sunbeam eliminating shadows.

"Hey, Doc," he mumbled, those green eyes braving the light before drifting closed again.

Wolf or not, J. D. Sumner was a patient whose knee had been carved into by her scalpel. Her compassionate heart—the same one Peter had inherited—softened.

She laid a cool hand across Sumner's forehead; found his pulse on the big freckled wrist resting on the blanket. Good—regular and strong. Skin a little warm but that was expected fresh out of the O.R.

Thank God. Another win.

Stop thinking like an intern! Focus on your patient.

She did. And saw he was a big man, long and lean and honed in all the muscled regions. She knew the human anatomy inside and out. Eleven years of school, orthopedic studies and her residency had garnered her that knowledge. Sumner was the epitome of health.

"The surgery was a success," she told him quietly, her hand slipping upward to stroke back his hair.

He had wonderfully thick hair, McDreamy-shaggy and a dark auburn hue she'd sell a kidney for. Rich was all she could think. The color was rich as a forest of oaks in autumn.

Forests again. What was the matter with her? She wasn't even an outdoor kind of gal.

"Feels good, Doc." His words came less slurred; his eyes slowly zeroed on her. "Your fingers are nice and cool."

God, what *was* she doing? She snatched back her hand, but not before his lips curved in a slight smile and a current landed in her abdomen. "The nurses will take you to your room in about fifteen minutes," she told him. "You'll need to wear the knee brace for a few days to keep the leg straight. I also want you to use crutches until you can put pressure on the leg without pain."

He was having trouble keeping his eyes open. "Can I have some water? Mouth feels dry as Arizona."

"The recovery nurse will give you a few sips." For anyone else she would have complied. But there was something about J. D. Sumner that confused her, sent tingles up her arms wherever she touched him. The moment he'd come into the E.R., snow-covered and biting his lip, she had felt that electricity. Thankfully, during surgery her focus had been too intense.

"No, you," he said. "I want you to—"

"Yolanda can—"

"Please." He caught her hand in a shocked move. "You."

"Mr. Sumner, I have other patients."

"J.D. It's…J.D."

In his eyes she saw that same flicker of apprehension she'd noticed before the operation. For some reason NHC's top man was afraid. But of what—hospitals in general? Was that why he hadn't had his knee fixed years ago? Oh, yes, she'd noted the old damage, the 'jumper's knee.' Why had he ignored the problem so long?

Again, her heart responded. While fear often accompanied patients and families into the hospital, Ella worked hard to ease their situations. J. D. Sumner was no different.

"All right," she said and nodded to the nurse tucking a warming blanket around his feet. Within seconds, Yolanda handed Ella a plastic water bottle and straw.

Gently she slid her hand beneath his head—fingers automatically weaving through the density of his hair—and lifted him to the flexible straw. His lips were well-shaped, though dehydrated from the anesthetic. Dark whiskers covered his top lip and obstinate jaw, and flowed down his neck to his Adam's apple.

As a kid he would've had freckles across his cheeks.

Sipping slowly, he watched her watch him and again she felt that prickle in her belly. Gold dusted his irises, but most surprising were his lashes: black and long, curvy as a seashell. To achieve what he grew naturally, she'd need extra-lash mascara.

"Thank you," he said hoarsely.

She slipped her hand free of his head, set the bottle on the rolling tray. "You're welcome. Yolanda will look after you now."

"Will I see you again?"

"In about an hour. Meantime, try and sleep." She gave him what she hoped was a reassuring smile. "You'll be up before you know it."

She turned to go.

"Doc? I'm sorry for last night. What I said. About the throbbing."

"No offense taken. Sometimes pain will make people say strange things." Which was true.

"You're Peter Wilder's sister."

"I am."

His dry lips worked up a semi-smile. "Much prettier to look at. But…this won't stop me from moving NHC's agenda forward."

Of course it wouldn't. "Mr. Sumner. I have larger issues to worry about than what's up your sleeve."

His gaze touched her bare arm. "Cute arm up *your* sleeve."

"Later," she said. But his look felt like a touch of his big hand.

"The pretty lady blushes."

Shaking her head, she left recovery vexed he could knot her tongue with less than a handful of words. With just a look. *Get ahold of yourself, Ella. You're a doctor and he's…he's a patient!*

And the most virile man she'd seen in years.

Lord, the mere length of his eyelashes had her heart in arrhythmia. Oh, yes. One look from him and her palms sweated as though she sat behind the hottest boy in ninth grade—instead of being the accomplished doctor she was and a woman of almost thirty.

And still a virgin, Ella. Let's not forget that.

The thought of celebrating her next birthday in another maiden voyage had her shuddering.

Dammit. Four years ago she should have worked harder to coax Tyler out of his issues of impotency and away from thinking he wasn't a "whole" man because he sat in a wheelchair. However, she'd been so busy interning she'd let them fall into a platonic relationship. Which in itself was a revelation. She hadn't truly loved Tyler as a woman should. She'd loved him as a friend.

Perhaps, if they'd had sex… Who was she kidding? She'd chosen him as a safety net—one that kept her focused on her honors status rather than her status as a woman.

Still, had they had some form of sex she'd be more suave today, more adept around the J.D.'s of the world.

Pretty. His word swirled in her mind. She'd never considered herself pretty. Anna, her sister, was the pretty one. No, the *beautiful* one with the white-blond hair and lovely blue eyes.

If J. D. Sumner saw Anna, he wouldn't look a second time at Ella with her plain brown eyes, the straight dark hair she hacked off the instant it closed in on the collar of her lab coat.

Be grateful for what you've got Ella.

And she was grateful. For many things. Her siblings. This hospital, founded on the ethics and standards of her late father. Her family's resources to send her to university. Her intelligence.

So…why couldn't she be grateful *and* pretty?

She gave herself an inner shake. She didn't have time for this—this silly vanity. She'd taken the Hippocratic oath, for God's sake. Nothing mattered but her skill. She had no time to think about J.D. and the experiences he had with beautiful women.

So she told herself…every spare second of her shift.

Chapter Two

At 8:00 p.m. that night she pulled her Yaris into her garage from the back alley and shut off the ignition. Bone-tired, she sat listening to the engine tick. The car had been her father's last birthday gift, a month before his retirement—and untimely death.

She remembered the massive red ribbon on the hood, the gigantic card with *Happy 29th, Ella! Love always, Dad* on the driver's seat.

Her eyes stung. Never again would she see her barrel-chested daddy, hear his kind voice, feel his big bear-paw hands stroke her hair or rub her shoulder affectionately.

That birthday had been the best. Sometime during the night, he'd driven the car into her garage and had her beatup Chevy removed. Then he'd rung her doorbell at five in the morning, an hour before her shift at the hospital. He'd stood there on her little porch with a cup of Starbucks in one hand and *The Boston Globe* in the other. And the biggest grin.

The early morning sun dappling his gray hair, he'd led her through her little backyard, with its grand old maples, to the garage, saying he needed a ride to the hospital because he'd cabbed it to her house to wish her a happy birthday.

And there sat the little blue Yaris.

Ah, Daddy. I hope you know I miss you like crazy.

Sighing, she hit the remote for the garage door before climbing from the car with a sack with homemade clam chowder from Prudy's Menu, a deli she frequented when she worked overtime.

Tugging her wool-lined coat tight around her, she headed across the snowy, moonlit backyard for the rear door of her small Cape Cod house, the one her maternal grandmother had lived in for sixty-two years and bequeathed to Ella and Anna three years ago. From the start, Anna hadn't wanted the house, but Ella vowed to buy out her half by setting up an account and depositing monthly increments in her sister's name.

As she stepped inside her quaint country kitchen, a squeaky meow greeted her before a three-legged bundle of gray fur came around the corner. A year ago, Ella had found the wounded kitten on the side of a highway, and brought her home to heal.

"Hey, Miss Molly." She cuddled the animal close. "Smell the soup, do you? Let's find you some nice tuna instead."

At nine, she turned out the kitchen lights and headed down the hall to take a bath. Oh, but she was tired.

Today had been a grueling one. Ice on the highways resulted in two traffic accidents, causing broken legs, a shattered shoulder and a fractured spine. Then there was the man shoveling snow off his roof who'd fallen to a cement patio, smashing both heels.

And of course, J. D. Sumner with his damaged knee.

She had popped into his room before leaving the hospital. Why she'd left him until last on her evening rounds, she couldn't say. Normally, she checked each patient room-by-room, ward-by-ward.

But she'd gone to check the roof faller first before backtracking to room 239—one of only three private rooms in the hospital.

Nothing but the best for the executive of Northeastern HealthCare, she thought wryly.

Eyes on the small muted TV, cell phone attached to an ear, he'd been resting comfortably when she entered the room.

Finally, I get some attention, he'd grumbled after ending the call. His sensual lips quirked and between his lashes there lay a gleam. *Heard you in the corridor,* he'd gone on. *Either you were afraid to come into my room or I'm your favorite patient and you saved the best till last.*

At that, she laughed. She couldn't help it. Despite his helplessness in that hospital bed, the man had an impossible ego. She explained that his room was near the exit— at which he'd chuckled and called her a fibber.

The banter continued for several moments before she

examined his surgery, checked his blood pressure, pulse and temperature. And then he asked, *Why are you doing the nurse's job?*

Why, indeed? she thought now, letting herself slide beneath the steamy water for a moment before rinsing out her hair.

How could she characterize her father's legacy to a man geared to implementing the type of corporate practices armed to decimate the care of WRG? Practices that filed a patient under a number rather than a name, that sent patients home with little more than a fare-thee-well.

So the rumors went.

James Wilder was the reason she'd gone into medicine. His compassionate teachings were entrenched in Ella. She would not give them up. Not even if the hospital board decided to accept NHC's takeover bid, should it come to that. Which she desperately hoped would never happen.

The water grew cool and she pulled herself lethargically out of the tub. Molly offered a squinty-eyed look from the mat by the sink.

Ella laughed. "Yeah, I know. Nothing riveting." No, Anna was the family beauty queen. Elegant, lovely and gifted. *Oh, Anna. I miss you.*

With a sigh, Ella pulled the tub's drain. Maybe one day they would be close again—as sisters should be.

The phone rang. The nightstand clock read nine twenty-eight and caller ID indicated the hospital. Although she wasn't on call, she became immediately alert, and lifted the receiver. "Dr. Wilder."

"It's Lindsey, Doctor."

The night nurse.

"Your patient, Mr. Sumner, is reacting to the Demerol, I believe. Heart's pounding, sweats, woozy."

She climbed from the bed, reached for her clothes. The symptoms definitely sounded like a reaction. "Temp and BP?"

"Fifty-two, and seventy over sixty. Feels as if he's about to pass out."

Damn. His admission form hadn't signified any allergies. "Get two liters of saline into him, flush it out. Now. And get Doctor Roycroft in to check his stats." Roycroft was on night call. "I'll be there in a few minutes."

She hung up, rushed into her jeans and a sweatshirt. She didn't stop to think why she needed to race to his bedside. The nurses and on-call doctors were there.

They're competent, Ella. You're not dealing with an alcoholic nurse who wouldn't acknowledge her own problems.

Still, she couldn't take the chance. This time *she* was responsible, not a scrub nurse. *She* had prescribed the meds.

In her car, she shivered, although the vents blasted hot air. At the hospital, she half-jogged up the stairs to the second floor.

A male nurse inputting computer data sat behind the counter of the floor station. "Is Lindsey with Mr. Sumner?" she asked.

The man glanced up from the screen. "No, but the patient is okay, Doctor. We got him settled. Changed his nightshirt and the sheets. Sponged down his skin."

Ella scanned Sumner's chart. Heart and blood pressure back to normal. Saline doing its work. "Thank you. I'll check on him while I'm here." She headed down to the room.

A nightlight glowed from the opposite wall, casting a dim hue across the bed and J.D.'s form under the blankets. His leg had been propped on several pillows. He was still awake.

"Hey, Doc," he said, voice deep and raspy. "You come all the way back just to see me?"

Sick as he'd been, she heard the grin in the tone, pictured his grass-green eyes in the dark.

"How are you feeling?" she asked, automatically checking the pulse along the arch of his elevated foot for circulation. *Steady.*

"Wasn't feeling so hot a while ago."

"You reacted to the Demerol. Were you aware about the symptoms before, by chance?"

"No. Never bother with meds unless it's aspirin or some such. Don't like taking prescription meds. Don't need 'em."

She wanted to ask about his jumper's knee. He hadn't gone without pain at some point in his life. But he was drowsy and he'd been through enough for one night. "You may need a medical alert bracelet for the Demerol." Setting a palm against his forehead, she noted the coolness of his skin. He was okay.

"Get some rest, Mr. Sumner."

"I wish…" His eyes drooped. "I wish you'd call me J.D."

She ignored the request. J.D. was far too personal. It gave him an edge she wasn't prepared to relinquish.

"Sleep, sir. It's best for your injury. Let the saline and the medication do its job."

"They gave me Tylenol 3."

"It'll help with the pain." And the fever. "I'll see you in the morning."

"What time?"

"Around seven."

"I pressed the call button right away," he said, as if reluctant to let her go. "Was surprised someone attended so fast."

"That's how our hospital works. No calls go unnoticed or unattended. Here, patient care is first and foremost."

"Good." His breathing slowed, his eyes drifted closed. "Wish you were on call. I hate…hospitals."

"Well," she said softly, "I hope you won't hate ours too much."

"'Ni', Doc."

"Goodnight."

She left his room, returned to the nurses' station and wrote her observations on his chart. Several minutes later she was heading home, hands gripping the steering wheel. Would she ever get past the horrifying repercussions of that surgery in Boston?

One day at a time, the counselor had told her.

God help her if something had gone wrong with J. D. Sumner.

He's already scared. The thought popped up like a weed.

Oh, he had a cocky attitude, but an underlying current of apprehension rode his voice from the moment Mike

O'Rourke, one of the hospital's paramedics, brought him into the E.R. Which, she supposed, was understandable, but still…

In her mind she backtracked the past two days. His constant questions, the hint of anxiety. His need for her at his side. And it was more than simple attraction. He saw her as his lifeline. Why?

Why was J. D. Sumner, executive of one of the largest health care corporations, leery of hospitals?

Or was it just *her* hospital?

J.D. woke in a cold and drenching sweat.

The hospital gown stuck to his clammy skin and for a moment his brain didn't register his surroundings. And then his eyes focused.

He lay in the hospital, a place he had not spent one night—never mind two—since his birth. The clock radio read 12:03 a.m. He'd been asleep less than two hours. His mouth tasted of dryer lint. He reached for the water, took a sip. The ice had long since melted.

Someone had placed the call button within reach, tying it to the guardrail near his hand. He pressed the red glow light of the tiny plastic knob—one, two, three. Shudders rolled through his body.

Within ten seconds, a soft tread came down the corridor. A woman entered his room.

"Doc?" J.D. rasped, eyes blurry.

"It's Lindsey," the woman said. "The night nurse. Are you okay, Mr. Sumner?"

"I'm soaked." His teeth rattled. He tried to focus, but

she stood etched in the dim glow from the hallway. "Need the doc," he slurred.

At his bedside, the nurse ran gentle fingers down his arms, took his cold hands between her palms. "I'll get you a clean gown and some extra blankets," she said, then disappeared.

J.D. shivered. He hadn't been this cold since he'd been a kid and had to shovel his dad's truck out of a ditch one bitter winter night when the old man hit an icy patch and plowed into the snowdrift along the shoulder of the road. *I'm frozen,* he'd told his dad.

You're not shoveling hard enough, Pops had retorted.

Another shudder rushed through J.D.'s body.

Lindsey returned with blankets in her arms, a fresh water bottle in her hand and the male nurse on her heels.

"We'll get you comfy in no time, Mr. Sumner," she said.

Gently, they assisted him from bed to a chair. And while Lindsey changed the linens, the man changed J.D.'s nightshirt. Minutes later he lay snug and dry under the covers. His knee throbbed like a son of a bitch.

While he sipped water, Lindsey took his pulse and inserted an ear thermometer. She had calm hands and a soothing voice. He'd always imagined hospitals as semi drug-induced prisons where the injured were at the mercy of emotionless medical staff who pretty much wanted you out of the way and not holding up the assembly line.

The type of hospitals NHC praised. For some reason, tonight the standard felt false.

Checking his stats, Lindsey asked, "How's the knee?"

"Feels like it's been run over by a truck."

"We'll give you some more Tylenol."

His breathing eased. "Is the doc coming?"

"We've called her, but it's just the Demerol working itself out of your system."

After he'd taken the pills, the nurse tucked him in as if he were a child. "You'll sleep now," she said kindly.

He damn near expected her to kiss him goodnight on his forehead, but she stepped back and drew up the guard-rail. "Good night," she whispered.

He was too tired to respond. Already the pills were spreading their smooth serenity into his raw knee and his last thought was that he couldn't remember anyone ever tucking him in at night.

Definitely not his old man.

The wind had died down by the time Ella drove through the cold dawn to the hospital the next morning. All night, between bouts of sleep, she'd worried about Sumner. Considering Lindsey would have notified her if something had gone awry, forfeiting sleep had been silly and foolish. *Sheesh.* If she thought of the thousands of lost nights during her studies and internship….

Pulling into her parking spot, she inhaled hard. If she hadn't been so driven, so fevered over getting her medical degree, maybe there would have been someone after Tyler….

Oh, God. The last thing she needed was to remember Tyler. Dear Tyler with his brilliant medical mind. His broken body after his skiing accident in their first year of internship. Tyler whom she had loved, but hadn't been *in love* with. Until he was gone, dead of acute pneumonia, and she cried and despaired and regretted.

More for him or for you, Ella?

The thought stopped her cold at the door of the change room.

Be honest. Tyler hadn't wanted to live. He hadn't been able to surrender his dreams of neurosurgery.

All right. The tears were more for me.

Her conscience shaken, she pushed into the room. As always, changing into her scrubs and lab coat made her a doctor once more. No time for regrets or moaning over lost chances.

She walked to the nurses' station and collected her charts, scanning each of the seven patients requiring her attention. J.D., she noted, hadn't slept well initially according to Lindsey: *Cold sweats, shivers, dry mouth. 9:35—Changed Demerol to T3. 24:03, paged Dr. E.W.—Changed bedding/gown. Patient repeatedly asked for Dr. E.W.*

That his temperature rose a half degree after a restless night was normal. His vitals overall were good. She reread *repeatedly asked for*, glanced down the hallway to 239 and her heartbeat quickened. He was okay. The remainder of the night had been uneventful. She wondered if he was awake, if he'd eaten breakfast, if he waited for her.

She began her rounds. Each patient received her personal attention, each received encouragement for healing. These were the ethics her father had taught that made WRG a hospital where patients could heal in comfort and ease. *Patients are people.* She could almost hear her father's voice. *They have faces and names. They are not medical terms.*

She walked into J.D.'s room with her dad smiling over her shoulder. "How are we this morning, Mr. Sumner?"

He was sitting up in bed, knee raised by pillows, his hair falling endearingly over his forehead—and with a sex appeal that seared like a flame.

God, he was a striking man. All the studying, all those late, late nights when she'd propped her eyes open with toothpicks and drank coffee until her back teeth floated…none of it prepared her for *this*. For J. D. Sumner.

Her next breath snagged at the flash of his smile. "Hey, there, Doc. Can you get me out of here this morning?"

On the pretense of checking his chart, she walked to his side. "You had a bit of a tough night."

"Nothing I couldn't handle."

"Mm-hm." She pressed two fingers against his wide, warm wrist. Heart rate steady, strong and slower than yesterday. "Do you exercise regularly, Mr. Sumner?" she asked, examining his knee for discoloration and swelling.

It took her a moment to realize he hadn't replied. Ella lifted her head. Eyes dark and deep as jungle pools stared back.

"Why won't you call me by my first name?" he asked quietly.

"It's better this way." *First names are too close and personal.*

A chuckle. "Ah…got it. Better for *you*. Interesting."

"Not interesting, professional."

At that he laughed. "Now there's a fun word coming from one of this hospital's finest. In my world, professional comes with proficiency and competence."

"And we're not?" she asked mildly.

"Oh, you're professional, don't get me wrong. You just need to speed things up a little. Not do so much hand-holding."

She ignored his critique. "Hold as still as possible, I want to change the bandages. Then later this morning we'll get you up and around for a few minutes. And for your information, professionalism is at the top of our agenda, particularly when it comes to patient care." She shot him a stern look. "Which your company doesn't seem to understand, from what I hear."

"My company understands you would do well to update equipment, move into the modern world. Why work with old tools, old standards, if new ones are at your fingertips?"

She tossed the bandages in the trash bin by his bed. "God forbid, I ever need medical care in an NHC-run hospital. I'd be a faceless, nameless entity."

"You'd be cared for in the most resourceful, sophisticated way possible."

Ella paused, her eyes locking on his. "Have you received any *un*sophisticated medical attention since you were admitted, J.D.?"

She realized her error the instant his name left her tongue and his grin bloomed big as a kid's on the last day of school.

"Now, *that* sounds perfect," he said, much too brash for her liking. "A little culture, a little smokiness, a little se—"

"Stop right there."

"I was going to say—"

"Do not go there."

"—sensitivity." Another broad grin. "Ah. You thought I had something else on my mind."

Despite his injury, the man was relentless. And he read her too well. "What you have on your mind is not my concern."

"That a fact?"

"Absolutely. My interest in you, Mr. Sumner, falls into one category. You are my patient. Nothing else."

He sighed with flair. "You break my heart, Ella."

Oh, boy. She had to force herself to remember that he'd been in the board meeting the other night representing Northeastern HealthCare. He could possibly eradicate everything Walnut River General stood for. Which meant he could not, in any way, be trusted.

His flirtations were a guise, a smoke screen to obtain information to sink her hospital. The hospital her father had worked all his life to uphold with integrity and dedication—and above all—class-A skills and leadership. Shifting the subject, she placed her fingers on his knee and hiked her chin toward the S-shaped birthmark on the inside of his thigh. "Who gave you the birthmark?"

"Probably some ancient ancestor."

"Do you have family in Walnut River?" She moved her fingers around his kneecap.

"Why?"

"I have another patient with the same birthmark."

His leg jerked. "Take it easy," he breathed.

Concerned, she touched the area where her fingers had been. "This hurt?"

"It's sensitive."

Leaning closer, she examined the region below the knee. "Hmm. It shouldn't be. It's too far from the incision." Beyond the small line of stitches, his knee appeared normal in its healing. No signs of blood poisoning, thankfully.

Ella pressed the call button. "I'll prescribe a topical cream."

"Now?" J.D. asked, suddenly serious. His gaze searched his injury, his Adam's apple bobbed.

For a moment Ella was tempted to reverse her call to the nurses' desk and ease the nervousness his tone carried. "Everything's fine, but a nurse will finish up here so I can continue my rounds."

"Will you be back later?"

June Agger, a twenty-year veteran with the hospital, entered the room. "Dr. Wilder?"

"Could you finish dressing Mr. Sumner's surgery for me, June? Thanks." To J.D., she said, "I'll be back when I do rounds tonight. We're going to keep you an extra day to monitor your meds, make sure nothing else causes you fever and nausea. If you need me for anything concerning your knee, June will know where to find me. Meantime, Ashley, our physiotherapist, will begin some passive and very mild ambulatory exercises. Don't overdo it, though."

"Doc," he called before she made it out the door. "The day can't go fast enough."

Until she returned to him.

She headed down the hallway, convinced danger was spelled J.D.

Except for the octogenarian dozing at the tiny desk near the door, the hospital library was empty at three in the afternoon.

Dressed in a blue terry robe and using the crutches the physiotherapist prescribed, J.D. quietly thumped his way across the hardwood floor. The library was elementary-sized. Ten inner shelves were stacked with fiction and two walls held reference, research and an assortment of current magazines.

Situated in the northwest corner of the hospital's ground floor, the library had a cozy nook facing two corner windows where patients could enjoy the hospital gardens now under three feet of snow.

Gingerly, he sank into a cushiony chair. Beyond the glass, a variety of trees—elm, oak and maple, New England's finest—were scattered across the gardens. He'd read about them in a brochure at the information desk four hours before he busted up his knee. Which at the moment throbbed like an insane drum behind the brace.

Too much damn walking, he thought. Hadn't she told him not to overdo it? Mercy, but he wanted out of here. He wanted to get back to his job, back to New York. He wanted out of Walnut River.

Barely loud enough to be discerned, the PA system called "Dr. Ella Wilder, recovery three. Dr. Ella Wilder, recovery three."

He pictured her hurrying to the patient, her pink Nikes quick and quiet on the tiled floor, a worry line between her fine dark brows. He imagined her slim hands on the patient's forehead, taking his pulse, her voice—the one with smoke and sex rolled into its vowels—a balm to distressed nerves.

J.D. smiled. Oh, yeah. *Sex.* She'd read him well this morning. She, with the keen mind, perceptive eyes and beautiful face. Ella Wilder had a sensuality that shot a man's testosterone sky-high.

Unfortunately, such women were out of his league. The type he attracted was brash and bold. Women who knew how to have a good time, if not for a long time. Women who knew how to let him take what he needed, what he wanted. Without frills. Without obligations and assurances and emotional morasses.

A deep disillusionment crept in. Out over the gardens a soft fall of snow had begun and he felt it burying what he'd always known. No matter how hard he scraped and clawed his way through the maze of life, the ghosts of his blue-collar past would forever haze his heels.

And a woman like Ella Wilder, with her culture and sophistication, with her background smacking of old money, heritage and long lines of tradition would see him as a mere speck on her chart.

Well, dammit, maybe it was time to make some alterations to that speck. And maybe, just maybe, it was time for him to be a different kind of man.

One the good doctor would appreciate.

Chapter Three

Whenever she could, Ella took lunch at home. The quiet of those sixty minutes helped her reenergize and refocus. Today was one of those days. She hadn't been able to get J.D. out of her head. The man dominated her thoughts during every lapsed moment. When she took a ten-minute water break. When she changed her scrubs from one surgery to the next. Thank God, the second she began scrubbing in her mind zeroed on her task.

This afternoon she had a single surgery scheduled. Eighty-year-old Mrs. Shipmen needed the radial head on her right elbow repaired. Ella looked forward to the surgery. She did not look forward to its completion. The afternoon would leave too much room for thoughts of J. D. Sumner.

Molly greeted her at the back door, purring happily as she twined around Ella's ankles.

She was standing at the window over the sink, eating the tomato and chicken salad sandwich she'd thrown together and musing about the snow she needed to clear from her walkway before dark, when her neighbor across the alley stepped out of his house and began sweeping his back stoop.

And suddenly it struck.

Jared Sumner. Best known for his gardening skills around Walnut River. Not only had he maintained the hospital's gardens, last summer she'd hired him to care for and nurture her property.

Six months before, she'd observed him limping around his backyard with a cane, so she had gone across the alley to inquire about his health. The old man had shrugged off her questions—until unbearable pain drove him to see her.

Last October she replaced his left hip. And asked about the birthmark on his inner thigh.

The S-shaped birthmark she queried J.D. about this morning.

Who gave you the birthmark?

Probably some ancient ancestor.

And then he'd felt pain. In a spot that should not have been painful. Surely, it hadn't been a ruse to sidetrack her?

Over the sink, she brushed the crumbs from her hands. "Wait here, Molly-girl. I'll be right back."

Ella shrugged into her coat, then headed out the back door. The cold air bit her lungs as she half-ran, half-strode, coat flying behind her, across the alley, through Mr. Sumner's back gate and across his tiny yard, a yard that in summer was an Eden.

A yard J.D. had played in—if the man on the stoop with the bristly outdoors broom was whom she believed.

The old gent raised his head as she came up the walkway he had yet to clear. "Hello, Mr. Sumner," she called.

"Doc." He straightened to his full height, a height equaling J.D.'s. and, leaning on the broom's handle, waited for her to halt below the stoop's four narrow steps. "Ya done for the day?" he asked, his Boston accent thick as the snow in his yard.

"I go back in about twenty minutes." She glanced at the broom. "Thought one of the high school kids was clearing your walks and steps." If she sounded exasperated it was because she could well imagine the old guy flying off those steps, arms and legs windmilling.

Like J.D. had.

"Huh," he grunted. "Damn kid doesn't know what the hell he's doin' half the time. Leaves the snow piled so close to the walk, all it does is slide back down."

She went up the stairs. "Give me that broom, please, and go on inside where I know you won't fall on your keester."

"Don't you mean my ass?" he grumped, though a smile lay in his voice.

"Whatever." She took the broom, and waved him toward the door. "I'll see you shortly."

"What for?"

"I have some questions to ask. Now, are you going to let me finish this or are you going to stand in the way?"

"Huh," he said again. "I've a mind to lock you out. Don't need a li'l mite like you naggin' my head off."

"I don't nag. It's called TLC. But you wouldn't know what that means, would you?"

"Fresh-mouthed doctor, is what you are," he griped, shutting the door in her face.

She swept the stoop and stairs, then grabbed the snow shovel parked against the house and tackled the walkway.

The door opened. "Do a good job—or I won't let you do it again." The door slammed shut.

Old coot, she thought, unable to resist the affectionate laugh that erupted. He'd been her neighbor since she moved into her grandmother's house a week after she finished her residency last year. After her grandmother's death three years before, renters had lived in the place—and neglected the property.

Mr. Sumner Senior had jumped at the chance to fix up her "pig sty," as he termed it. His labor didn't come cheap, but then a first-class groundskeeper was worth every penny she put in his pocket.

Finished with the walkway, she set the shovel in its spot and climbed the steps. She had all of five minutes.

After brushing the snow from the hem of her long woolen coat, she knocked once. As though he'd been waiting on the other side, he flung open the door.

"Thank you." Ella strode in. The kitchen's warmth stung her cold cheeks. She looked past the man to the interior and saw a small tidy room. He was as meticulous here as he was with the outdoors.

"I thought you had people to dice," he grumped,

gripping his carved wooden cane. "You're takin' up my afternoon."

"And you're welcome for the walkway."

A grunt.

She shoved her cold hands into the deep pockets of her coat and studied him a moment. Except for his height and thick silver hair, he looked nothing like J.D. Could she be mistaken? Oh, she understood that by asking specific questions she'd be digging into a part of their lives that was not her business. She was both men's doctor. Not their priest, psychologist or social worker.

But there was that birthmark.

And the last name—as well as the first—marking father to son.

She stared into the old man's blue eyes. "I'll make this short, Mr. Sumner. Do you have family?"

He was taken aback. "What the hell concern is that of yours? First you come here bitchin' about my shovelin', then you storm into my house and now you're askin' questions that got nothin' to do with patient care."

She wouldn't back down. "Do you?"

"If you're askin' if I have kids the answer is no."

"No children?"

"Ya deaf, Doc?"

The tension ran from her shoulders and settled in her gut. The old man was lying. "I have a patient in the hospital right now. His name is J. D. Sumner from New York City—"

"Don't know nobody in New Yawk." Cane in hand, he turned away and shuffled to the kitchen table, a small sixties chrome-and-Formica affair with two red vinyl chairs.

Had J.D. sat there once?

Hanging the cane over the back of a chair, the old gent lowered himself into the one facing the window that overlooked his backyard, and it startled Ella that her own kitchen table mirrored an identical arrangement.

He said, "Go back to your hospital, Doc. I'm gonna take a nap, if you don't mind." Staring out at his snowy world, he began massaging his hip.

She stepped forward. "Are you in pain?"

"Nothin' I can't handle."

J.D.'s words.

"You're due for another checkup next week. I'll expect to see you in my office."

He turned suspicious eyes on her; eyes that had her thinking of J.D. when he lay on the stretcher in Emerge and asked what she planned for his knee.

"If I need pills, I'll call you."

Stubborn old cuss. "You do that," she said. She should leave well enough alone. But she couldn't. Her heart could not stand by without trying. "And if you're curious about my other patient…he's mid-thirties, has dark auburn hair. And," she said, pausing for effect, "brown eyes."

No reaction. The old gent continued his vigilance on the yard.

"All right," she said. "I'll go now." However, as she opened the door she heard him whisper a word. Had it been *green*? She slanted a look over her shoulder to be sure, but he sat in profile, his jaw pointing toward the winter landscape, his lashes unblinking.

Ella released a small sigh. "See you later, Mr. Sumner."

He remained motionless.

Stepping outside, she softly shut the door, and smiled.

In profile, Jared Sumner was the image of his son.

J.D.'s skin was on fire one minute, the next like he'd been dunked in the North Atlantic, his teeth chattered so hard. What the hell was going on with his body? He'd done the exercises the therapist told him to do and he'd walked the corridor most of the day, resting whenever the pain got a little touchy.

He glanced at the plate the dinner staff had brought, the chicken congealing in the gravy. It smelled good ten minutes ago, before a wave of heat swept his body and a migraine set up camp in his brain.

Pulling the covers to his neck, he let his eyes drift shut. Maybe if he slept for a bit he'd be okay.

Another shudder shook his body. *Dammit.* What the hell was the matter with him? All he'd done was a little damage to his knee, for Christ's sake. Nothing major.

Except his body had switched into betrayal mode.

A stickler for health—he watched what he ate, exercised daily, drank in moderation, had sex regularly—the fact he had no control over his anatomy's behavior at the moment did not endear J.D. to the hospital. Had *she* made an error during surgery? The way that quack doctor had with his mom? Had Dr. Ella gone into the wrong area? Used an unsterilized scalpel? He'd read of such things.

Your imagination is running amuck, J.D. You know she

did her job. The incision was neat and tidy. Hadn't he viewed that thin, red line each time she redressed it?

Tomorrow couldn't come fast enough. Tomorrow he was leaving, whether she liked it or not. He couldn't recall ever staying more than a couple of hours in a hospital. Now here he was again, heading toward his second day with his temperature a rising tide.

Maybe he should call a nurse.

Where was the call button?

God, he was cold….

"Dr. Ella Wilder, line one, Dr. Ella Wilder, line one."

She punched her office intercom.

"It's Lindsey from floor two, doctor."

The night nurse began her shift at five o'clock. Ella glanced at the slim-banded watch on her wrist. Six-thirteen. She'd been at her desk almost an hour and a half. No wonder her shoulders ached.

Lindsey continued, "Mr. Sumner in 239 has a mild fever again. Fluctuates between chills and sweats. My guess is he worked the leg too much today, but he won't admit it."

"Swelling?"

"There's some distension and redness. Temperature's one hundred. He's asking for you."

"I'll be there as soon as I can. Put the leg on pillows and pack the area in ice. Also, increase the antibiotics by ten milligrams. Has he eaten?"

"Said he wasn't hungry."

"Let's get the fever down. Then we'll get some food into him. Thanks, Lindsey."

"Anytime, Doctor. Um…" Pause. "He's quite adamant about seeing you."

Her heart kicked. "Did he say why?"

"No. He just seems a little agitated, like he's nervous about being here."

"Here, or hospitals in general?"

"He didn't say."

"All right, I'll finish ASAP and come down."

Ella ended the call. It wasn't that often a patient of hers ran a fever that high. She'd bet he'd gone overboard with the exercising. Routinely, at noon and four o'clock, if she wasn't in surgery, she checked with the nurses' station to see how her patients fared. J.D., she knew, was determined to leave tonight after her rounds.

Well, J.D. It seems you'll be with me another night.

The thought had no more entered her mind than she glanced around her office as though she'd spoken aloud. Lord, she needed to go home, soak in a hot bath and—

Oh, Ella. You can't win with those double entendres. Grabbing another patient file, she set to work. Fifteen minutes later, she took the stairwell down to the second floor; stopped at the desk.

"Is he sleeping, Lindsey?" she asked the nurse.

"No, but he's adamant about speaking with you." A glint entered the woman's eyes. "I think he has a crush on you."

Ella sighed. "It's the meds."

"Maybe we should cut back, considering the number of questions he asks about you." She winked.

One thing about hospitals, Ella realized early in her career, their gossip mills loved information about their medical personnel. Her brother Peter had been fighting off rumors since he and Bethany butted heads and then locked lips.

That gossip mill was why Ella chose a counselor who practiced in Springfield, twenty miles away. The last thing she needed was her past—those dreaded few days during her years of internship in Boston—sifting down WRG's corridors. Not even her family knew of the deep-seated guilt Ella harbored due to that one incident, or of the nightmares that still galloped into her sleep. Yes, she understood the fault of the incident was not hers. That the scrub nurse with her in the O.R. had been an alcoholic, had neglected to sanitize one of the instruments. And, yes, the woman lost her job over the whole awful situation.

But a little boy nearly died as a result of that nurse's disregard—a child under Ella's care, and on whom she'd operated with an instrument she trusted and believed to be sterile.

And though she still fought to regain the confidence she'd once possessed as a doctor, it *was* returning, growing stronger day by day within the walls of her beloved Walnut River General.

Picking up J.D.'s chart and ignoring Lindsey's comments, Ella headed for 239.

His glassy green eyes fastened on her the instant she stepped around the door. "Finally," he said.

Taking the ophthalmoscope from her pocket, she went to his side, turned his face toward her, checked his pupils. "You're not my only patient, J.D."

"You called me J.D. again."

"Isn't that what you wanted?"

"There's a lot I want."

She ignored his look as she reached for the blood-pressure cuff hooked on the wall above his head.

"And," he added, voice indistinct with fever, "I usually get it."

Ella pumped the cuff. "Not all of us are so lucky."

A corner of his mouth worked. "We talking about the same thing, Doc?"

Oh, she understood precisely what he meant. What surprised her was his ability to tease while a fever warred inside his body. He was a determined man. "Well, there's one thing you won't get," she said, releasing the cuff.

"You?"

"Since you've elevated your blood pressure and contracted a second fever, there will be no discharge until tomorrow."

His mouth sobered. "You're keeping me another night?"

Ella curled her hands around the guardrail and pulled it up. "How many times did you exercise today?"

"A few."

"More than the physiotherapist's recommendation?"

He looked askance; she noticed his chapped lips. "J.D.," she said, offering the bottle of ice water to him, "do you know what it means to rest?"

"'Course. I do that at night."

"Not just at night. During the day, too. After any surgery your body needs time to heal, to redefine itself, so to speak. There's a lot going on inside you that requires your patience—and rest. In other words, I want you to empty your mind of work and whatever else is on your BlackBerry. While exercising prevents clots—" his eyes, she noticed, sharpened "—going beyond the recommended sessions has aggravated your injury. It's not going to get you back to your office quicker. And while your fever isn't off the charts, it is high enough to tell me your body has put up a red flag. So, until we get it down and stabilized for at least twenty-four hours, I can't discharge you."

During her speech, he sipped the water.

"Do you understand?" she asked.

He handed her the bottle. "I understand."

"Good." She set the water on the table and picked up the lip balm. "Keep your lips lubricated," she said, handing him the tube.

Fevered as his eyes were, the lightheartedness returned.

"To keep them from bleeding," she informed him, removing the ice packs. The swelling was there, more than she liked, but not as bad as she'd envisioned. By morning, he should be on the mend.

She assessed his circulation on the arch of his long narrow foot, and behind his anklebone where his skin was hairless and smooth and vulnerable.

"What's the rate?" he asked when she was done.

"Eighty-eight—normal with a fever."

"My resting pulse is fifty-four," he lamented.

"It'll be back once your temp decreases and you're healing." She gave him a smile. "You're in excellent shape." And he was. His calves were defined, his shoulders broad and solid. She'd noted the muscles in his forearms and biceps. No doubt another gym advocate. *Juice monkey* was Peter's description.

"Are you a member of a gym?" she asked.

"Hate gyms. I run, hike and row in the summer, snowshoe in the winter." He frowned at his leg. "I'd hoped to do some trails around here, maybe follow the river a few miles."

"No other sport injuries?"

"Nope." His eyes kept hers. "Maybe I *should* sue," he added, smearing his lips with the balm she'd given him. "For lack of viable fitness and fresh air—never mind my more, um, basic needs—all of which I'll sorely miss this month." His brows jumped twice and Ella suppressed the urge to roll her eyes.

"You are one predictable patient, Mr. Sumner."

He hissed. "Doc, Doc. How'm I to rescue my self-esteem after that comment?"

"I'm sure your self-esteem will hold out. I'll get Lindsey to change these ice packs in thirty minutes and then redress your leg."

From a narrow cupboard in the corner of the room, she retrieved a fresh, plump pillow.

"Meanwhile, I'll send up some soup so you'll have something in your stomach for the night. Lift up on your elbows." When he did, she removed the old pillow and tucked in the laundered one. "Better?" she asked when he'd resettled.

Something grazed his expression—like a butterfly's fleeting touch to a flower—and it curled around her heart the way the pillow she held wrapped his body's warmth around her hands. "I'll see you in the morning, J.D."

"Ella." Her name was soft on his chapped lips. "Thank you."

She touched the big hand resting on his chest. "You're welcome." Before she could draw away he gripped her fingers. "Can I see you?"

She pretended to misunderstand. "I need to finish my rounds."

"I meant after. Once I've left the hospital."

Carefully, she withdrew her hand from his clasp. "I seldom go to New York."

"I'll be staying in Walnut River for a couple weeks."

"Oh? So you do have family here?" Would he admit it now?

"Trying to get me offtrack, Doc? I'm asking if you'll have dinner with me once I'm discharged."

"Not offtrack. We just want to ensure—"

"Will you?" he asked, his throat so raspy she handed him the water bottle again.

"Let me think about it."

"Better than no, I suppose." He took a sip of liquid, eyed her. "I'll call you tonight." He flashed a smile. "You're in the phone book. I checked."

She shook her head. "I wonder how many other female nurses and doctors you've wooed." *For NHC.*

He didn't blink. "Not a one."

She huffed a laugh. "And I'll bet not for lack of trying."

"Don't have to try, Doc."

"Ah. Women drop like flies at your feet, then?"

A wicked grin. "Something like that."

"Good to know. Well, then." She lifted her chin. "Don't let me get in their way."

His laughter followed her out the door.

Chapter Four

J.D. checked his watch. Twenty minutes till nine.

Would Ella be up or in bed? While he liked the idea of her in bed, he hadn't liked the idea of her thinking he was shallow about women. Okay, he dated noncommittal types, those driven and married to their jobs, and he didn't savor that behavior in himself. But he had no clue how to act otherwise. He'd been raised to keep his emotions tightly reined.

Yes, by some stroke of luck, somewhere in his childhood he must have felt cared for, maybe even loved. Whatever smidgen he'd encountered, it stuck with him, gave him a lighter view of life, one in which he teased and cajoled and made goofy remarks.

And dumb-ass ones,

Women drop like flies at your feet, then?
Something like that.

As if she gave a damn about women fawning at his feet. Her dark eyes had laughed at him. Not with him, *at* him.

And he'd felt like the village idiot, pure and simple.

She was class through and through. Intelligent, lovely and most of all, a doctor who cared about her patients, and he'd treated her like one of his bar meets after a long board meeting.

He owed her an apology.

Dialing her number on his BlackBerry, he waited for the ring. One…two…three…four. She wasn't home—

"Hello?" A little breathless. As if she'd been rushing from the bath or from making a cup of tea or having sex—

"Hello?" she repeated, a hint of sharpness in her tone.

"It—" He cleared his raspy throat. "It's me."

"J.D." His name slipped like a breath into his ear and for a second he couldn't speak. "Are you okay?"

"I'm good," he assured, though his leg ached like hell, even with the painkillers she'd prescribed. "I wanted to apologize for my behavior earlier."

"Your behavior?"

She'd forgotten him. God, he *was* a fool. As if she had time to think of him. "When you came to check on my fever. I acted like an idiot." He gusted a breath of relief she hadn't hung up. "I'm not used to…" How to explain what he felt around her, these…*emotions*? "I'm not accustomed to doctors giving such thorough care," he finished lamely.

Not at all what he meant, but then every time he was

in her proximity his brain cells scattered like dandelion fluff in a spring breeze.

"You've never been in a hospital before, have you?"

"A few years back I cracked my elbow playing basketball."

"Thought you had no other sport injuries."

He chuckled. "I lied."

"Do you do that often?"

"What, play sports?"

"Lie."

The word punched. "No," he said. "Never."

"So you're honest as the day is long when you say things like not having to try around women."

He sputtered a laugh. "You don't forget much, do you, Doc? Guess I'd best watch what I say."

"Excellent idea," she said and he detected a hint of humor. "Women can read you like a book, Mr. Sumner. You're on page thirty-three."

"Ouch and ouch."

"Mm-hm. And here's a little tip. Don't tell a woman she looks pretty when in reality she looks like roadkill."

"Yikes. Is that worse than a bad-hair day?"

"Far worse."

"And you've known women who looked like roadkill?"

"I've *been* a woman who's looked like roadkill."

"Unbelievable. Cannot picture it."

"You haven't seen me after a seven-hour surgery."

"I'd give anything to see you after *any* surgery." And he meant it. She fascinated him.

She laughed, and he imagined those dark eyes soft in

the lamplight. "Not in this lifetime. Besides, if your fever stays down tomorrow, you'll be discharged, and on your way back to New York."

"I'm not returning to New York. Not right away," he added. "I'm taking a couple weeks off, staying in Walnut River."

"Oh?"

"*Oh*? How about, 'Oh, J.D. I'm so glad because I look forward to seeing more of you'?" he teased.

"If I see more of you," she retorted, "it would mean you're back in the hospital. And that would mean I didn't do my job right."

He glanced at his elevated leg, which nurse Lindsey had redressed after removing the ice packs. "You've done your job perfectly. The swelling is down." He hesitated. "I want to see you on a personal level, Ella. Have dinner with you."

"J.D., I'm your doctor, not your next conquest."

Her notion of him dug into a nerve. "Who the hell said anything about conquests? I'm asking you to sit across a table and have a meal and a bottle of wine with me. That's it."

"Can't happen."

"Can't or won't?"

"Both. Now I need to get some sleep and so do you. 'Night."

"Ella—dammit, wait!"

When he didn't hear the dial tone, his eyes closed in relief. "Thank you," he said quietly. "Look, I'll get to the point. I told you I don't lie and I don't. I'm attracted to you, all right? And I think it's there for you, too. Now, maybe I'm presumptuous, but I don't think so. I feel it every time you look at me. I'm familiar with a woman's response and—don't hang up because I'm not being arrogant. You treat me differently than other patients. You're reserved, you look away when our eyes meet, which intrigues me, Ella. You make me wonder. I've never wondered about a woman." Pressing a finger and thumb against his eyes, he said, "And I can't believe I'm making an absolute ass out of myself but there you have it."

Lungs laboring as though he'd run hurdles, he gripped the phone so hard his hand shook. *Hell*, he'd never been so nervous around a woman in his life. What was the matter with him?

For five slow heartbeats, silence. Had she hung up after all?

Then, "I'm not saying yes and I'm not saying no. I understand you want an answer tonight, but I can't give it."

"Okay." He could deal with that. After the litany he'd given, a *maybe* was more than he had expected. Maybe had possibility. Reams of possibility.

"However," she went on, "we will not discuss this again until the day of your discharge. Agreed?"

Which could be tomorrow. "Agreed."

"And J.D.?"

"Yeah?"

"What you just said?" Pause. "You're right." She hung up.

His smile was slow but strong. That maybe had just ballooned into a yes. And tomorrow was a whole new day.

* * *

He was eating breakfast when his BlackBerry indicated a text message from NHC. Grabbing the device from the side table, he snorted. Took his boss long enough. It had been three days since J.D. called the man and left a voice mail about his knee surgery.

Opening the message, he noted its subject: "Congratulations." J.D. frowned, read:

You've got the inside track. Perfect opportunity to observe hospital staff. Talk to administrator. He's easy to convince. Present case Feb. 26. –FJS

"Well, Frank Jerry Sorenson," J.D. muttered, closing the BlackBerry and picturing the bull-necked senior executive chairing the thirty-seat mahogany table in the New York boardroom like a kingpin. "Thanks for the heartfelt commiseration about my knee."

Should it surprise him?

'Course not. Frank was all business. If one of his grunts—which, even with his recent promotion, included J.D.—fell ill or caused a ripple in NHC's ever-widening pool of conquests, that grunt was either fired or demoted. J.D. could thank his fairy godmother that Frank considered his wrecked knee an opportunity. On the bright side, he'd keep his promotion and his position. And, seven years of slaving wouldn't be in the toilet.

Appetite lost, he pushed his breakfast tray aside and thought about the message he would return to Frank. *Sound enthusiastic. Don't let him think you're in pain or having a problem.*

"Problems" meant your fingers got squashed as the guy behind you took a giant step upward on the ladder of success. FJS hated problems. In other words, kiss butt—and imagine a raise.

He flicked open the BlackBerry, clicked Reply. *Done* he wrote. Frank drooled over cryptic notes that said precisely what he wanted to hear. J.D. closed the device just as Ella walked into his room, a smile on her pretty lips. His heart leapt.

"How's my patient this morning?" she asked, going straight for his foot, and pressing two fingers against his pedal pulse.

If she said *my* patient again, his tongue wouldn't work for a week. As it was he barely mumbled, "Much better, thanks."

"Good." She wrote her findings on his chart and he realized she wore her white lab coat over jeans this morning. "Rest and relaxation today, okay? No strenuous exercises. I don't want that fever back. And then tomorrow you're home free."

"You mean I'm in bed all day?"

She smiled. "All day."

"Doc, that sounds like a hell—heck—of an idea if it involved a woman, but—Whoa, the lady blushes. Now there's a unique sight."

A little laugh erupted. "Yes, I imagine it is for you."

"What's that supposed to mean?"

"It means…" She leaned forward, shone the eye gizmo in his left pupil; he could smell this morning's shower on her skin, in her hair. "That you're beyond redemption."

He clapped his chest. "You injure my sensibilities."

"Hmm." She looked into his right eye, but he caught

the hint of a grin—and damn near kissed it before she straightened to write on his chart. As she reached for the blood pressure cuff, he noticed her long, slim fingers, imagined them around other parts of his anatomy. For a moment, he closed his eyes.

"Hurt?" she asked.

He snapped to attention. "Huh?"

"Do you need a painkiller?"

Yeah, but not the kind she meant. "You available?"

Her eyes locked on his. Again a corner of her mouth twitched. She was laughing at him. He was in pain and she was laughing. "It's not funny," he grumbled.

"Let's have a peek at the knee, shall we?"

"Let's not." He squirmed under the covers, not wanting her to look at the spot on his leg barely twelve inches from his arousal....

Both her dark brows lifted. "Something wrong, Mr. Sumner?"

Oh, yeah, there was *something* all right. His erection. "J.D.?"

"Look, can we do it later?" *Great word choice, J.D.*

"Fine, I'll get June to redress your leg. When you're ready."

He caught her hand. "I want you." *No good, no good*.

She studied his fingers curled around her wrist and he forced himself to let go.

"That won't be possible," she said, as though the texture of her skin hadn't etched itself onto his palm. "This is actually my day off. Once I've finished rounds I'm heading back home."

"You're leaving me here all day—alone?" he asked, at last understanding why she wore jeans under that lab coat.

"I am."

His heart kicked into his throat. She was his lifeline. Knowing she was in the hospital made his day bearable. At night, she was less than twelve hours away. And if he called her that time was sliced to six hours. But an entire twenty-four hours while he had no idea of her whereabouts…?

"Ella, I…" *Hate hospitals. My dad hated hospitals. My mother died here. It's stupid, I know, but hospitals scare the hell out of me.*

"You'll be okay." She touched his hand, that quick re-assuring touch. Just as swift, he caught her fingers again.

"Don't—" *Don't leave me alone.* His chest burned with shame. Talk about instant deflation. He was a coward of the first degree. A wimp in a man's body. He wished he could control his fears. He hoped she wouldn't tell her colleagues. If FJS found out…

For a weighty moment, she let her hand remain under his. "J.D., is something wrong?"

Holding her gaze, he shook his head once.

Her hand slid from his. "Sure?"

"I'm fine." He mustered a grin. "Don't miss me too much, okay?"

A small bark of laughter escaped. "Don't consider yourself so important." At the door she hesitated, a soft smile on her lips. "You know, humility is a virtue I admire very much." Then she was gone.

J.D. stared at the empty doorway as the sounds of the

hospital returned—a trolley clattering with breakfast dishes; a page for Dr. Mason; nurses in the corridor, discussing an upcoming surgery…

Humility, she'd said. He was doomed. Humility wasn't in his repertoire of emotions. You didn't get to the top of the achievement ladder carrying a briefcase of humility.

Okay, she wanted him to be humble. Fine. Hadn't he decided to be a different man?

So if he gave it some thought he could, he supposed, reach a compromise, take that step toward change, toward…God help him…*humility.*

Feeling more at ease, he chuckled quietly. Of all the women he'd known—and he'd been familiar with a few—Ella was a puzzle he had absolutely no clue how to piece together.

He couldn't decide if that was bad or good.

Chapter Five

A light snow had begun to fall from slate-gray skies when Ella pulled into the church parking lot an hour before lunch. Already a small group hovered under the overhang of the side doors opening to the basement stairs. Below, the soup kitchen for Walnut River's homeless was in full swing.

After completing her residency at Massachusetts General Hospital in Boston, then returning to her hometown last summer, she'd been involved with the soup kitchen and its clientele. A number of the homeless were elderly, some intellectually disabled. Some had been on the streets for years, sleeping on sidewalks or in Dumpsters—sometimes through bitter winter nights—and prowling the city for handouts and drugs.

The church's minister, Rev. Oliver Blackwell, had referred Ella's first "street" patient two weeks after she began her practice at the hospital's medical clinic. Freddie Meikle was seventy-eight, an intellectually disabled man who had lived the streets for nearly thirty years. He had no family. Walnut River's sidewalks were home, the church's kitchen his dining table.

Ella had treated the old guy for severe arthritis in his knees and hands at Rev. Blackwell's request. The church offered a small stipend from their budget to cover some of the costs, but she'd refused. Instead, she had taken the case to Peter, who brought it to the board of directors. Two months later, with the aid of the hospital's Sunshine Fund, Ella capped Freddie's knees with plates.

Shutting off the car's motor, she saw the old guy wave and rush into the parking lot. His booted feet shuffled on the trampled snow and his thin shoulders drooped under his oversized army jacket.

"Hiya, Doctor Wilder," he called in his sweet, high voice. "You comin' to eat with us?"

"Sure am, Freddie. Do you know what's on the menu?"

"Uh-huh. Beef barley soup. It smells *goood*. I think Mrs. T made it."

Mrs. T. was Prudy Tavish, another of Ella's across-the-alley neighbors. Prudy lived next to Jared Sumner and, in partnership with her daughter, owned the delightful little deli called Prudy's Menu on Lexington Avenue, the main street of Walnut River. Each Sunday, she brought the day's homemade specialty to Rev. Blackwell's kitchen, and from the scent drifting through the side

vents, Freddie was right. Today she'd brought her wonderfully thick and tasty beef barley.

"Then I'm in luck," she said. "I'm starved as a bear."

Guffawing, Freddie fell into step beside Ella. "Ain't no
bears out now, Dr. W. They's hibernatin' in the mountains."

"Well, then." She smiled. "Guess I'm hungry as a
squirrel."

Another hoot. "Squirrels most likely in holes now, too.

They had reached the side entrance where several
other men and one woman she recognized stood, rubbing
their gloved hands and blowing white puffy breaths.

"Can we go in now, Dr. W?" Freddie's voice escalated
to a whine. "'S cold out."

"Hold on." She rang the buzzer.

"Hello?" the minister's voice came through the intercom.

"It's Ella Wilder, Reverend. May we come in?"

"Sure thing, Doc. How many so far?"

The question was the same every Sunday when she
rang the basement bell.

"Seven."

"Come on in, then."

A second later, the door buzzed. Ella waited for the
early birds to clomp down the stairs and line up at the end
of the kitchen counter where the food would be distrib-
uted within the next twenty minutes.

"Freddie," she called to the old gent clutching the stair
railing. "How are your fingers these days?" He continued to suffer from chronic arthritic joint pain, so Ella administered his medication via his long-time pal Rev.
Blackwell, whom Freddie saw twice a week.

"They're fine, Doc. No more pain."

They went into the spacious basement with its long tables and stacking chairs, ready for the lunch crowd.

"May I see?" she asked. "Just need to check for swelling."

Like a child, he stopped and removed his gloves, shoving them into his coat pockets. "See," he said, pointing to the twisted joint of his left middle finger and pinky. "Ain't near so bad no more."

She took his gnarled hands and examined each bony finger. The nails had grown unkempt over the past two weeks and grime lined the cuticles. She felt each knuckle, pressing gently, working her way across his hand and palm and probing the ulna bones in his dirt-rimmed wrists. He hadn't flinched and she was satisfied.

"I told you," he said, his grin wide and showing several gaps where teeth had once been.

She nodded. "You did, Freddie. Now, go wash your hands before you eat, okay?"

"Okay." He shuffled toward the rear of the basement and the washrooms.

Ella watched him go. He'd been one of her first patients as a licensed and certified doctor. For the rest of her life, she would remember him with tenderness in her heart.

Reverend Blackwell walked over. "Looks like we're getting a good crowd again."

"I wish we wouldn't," she said, watching more people come through the doors. "Because then we'd know they were kicking their drug addictions or were cared for by their families."

"Or dead," he said.

She smiled sadly. "That's not my option."

"Nor mine, Ella. How's Freddie?"

"Good. Fingers are actually starting to look normal again. The meds are helping. Did he get that coat from you?"

Oliver shook his head. "Prudy gave it to him. Was her husband's from the army."

Ella's cell phone rang. "Excuse me a moment." She pulled the phone from her shoulder purse. "Dr. Wilder."

"Ella." It was Peter. "Did you come in this morning?"

"Just to do a quick round. Why?"

"How many times have I told you to take time off when you *have* time off?"

"Did you call to check up on me again, big brother?" A grin tugged her lips.

"Not on your life." She heard him sigh. "Actually, I called to ask if you spoke with your patient, Mr. Sumner, this morning."

Immediately, she strode to the back of the room, to the women's washroom and the quiet there. "I checked his vitals. What's wrong?"

"Henry Weisfield came to see me."

Henry was the hospital administrator, the CEO of the institution's business and legalities, the man who oversaw all that went on in the belly of the medical community. He was also retiring in a few months—and he semi-favored NHC's takeover proposition. Scuttlebutt, however, indicated he lacked the faculties to make coherent decisions anymore and simply wanted to spend his last remaining years fishing, gardening and golfing. Not necessarily in that order.

"What did he want?" Ella asked, pushing through the door of the washroom. Thankfully, it was empty.

"He's given permission for one of NHC's people to observe the hospital's workings. Can you believe it?" He groaned. "Having NHC snooping around will be suicide."

"How so?" She checked her face in the mirror. The collar of her black, woolen coat nudged the hem of her hair. Time for a cut. She turned away and leaned her fanny against the sink's counter. "We don't have anything to hide. Let the guy check around for a day or two. All he'll see is a great hospital with a fantastic staff."

"The whole thing smells of rat dung."

"Paranoia doesn't look good on you, Peter. Give a little. What's Bethany say?"

"Says Weisman doesn't much give a damn and why should he? In a couple months, he'll be hitting the golf course. Meantime, he's not rocking the boat. Plus, he's half in favor of NHC taking over."

So she'd heard, but hadn't had the time to really sit down and analyze the hospital administrator's viewpoints. "Who are they sending?" she asked.

"The pigeon's already in place."

A chill ran up her spine. Only one fitted the bill. "J. D. Sumner."

"Correct."

"But you knew about his proposal—or NHC's—four days ago. And his knee injury was not done on purpose, Peter. I can't believe you'd think that way."

"Of course not. The injury was an accident, but I don't think he was sent here on a whim. He's been recently promoted and they want to see what kind of bacon he can bring home."

Ella hated slotting J.D. in that role. He seemed like a nice person, funny—albeit a little stuck on himself where women were concerned. But... "How can you be so sure?" she asked Peter. "Is that what Weisfield said?"

"I did some digging."

She didn't want to know what his digging had uncovered or who had helped. Or why he'd dug into J.D.'s history in the first place.

"I hear he likes you," her brother said offhandedly.

"I hope most of my patients like me," she shot back.

"I meant as a woman."

"Then you're listening to hospital gossip."

"So it's true?"

She laughed, but it sounded hollow and...a little cross. "Come on, Peter. You know better than to listen to the grapevine."

"There's never smoke where there isn't fire," he countered.

"Now you're quoting Mom." Their mother had died five years ago of cancer. Ella felt her loss still; some nights she mourned her parents and longed for the days when they had laughed and joked and sat at Christmas and Thanksgiving dinners, when each offered wisdom in their own way. Alice Wilder had loved quotes.

Peter said, "She had a point. Just be careful, Ella. That's all I'm saying."

"Fine, you've said it."

"Okay. I'll let you get back to the soup kitchen. Holler if you need another pair of hands down there."

"We're good. See you later." They hung up.

The washroom door swung open and a young woman, bundled in two coats and a knitted red hat, entered. Recognizing her, Ella smiled and turned on the sink's tap to wash her hands. "Getting crowded out there, Mavis?"

"'Bout fifty, maybe more."

"Have you decided to try detox?" she asked without preamble, knowing addicts could vanish in a blink of an eye.

The woman cast a furtive glance at the door. "Maybe."

"I know someone who can get you help," Ella went on casually.

"Okay." Clearly Mavis wanted to escape, either into a stall or out the door.

"Her name is Isobel Suarez." Ella turned on the hand dryer. "She's a friend of mine and a really nice person."

Mavis shifted from one foot to the other.

"If you want me to introduce you, tell Reverend Blackwell."

Mavis slipped into a stall. The conversation was done. "Bye, Mavis," Ella said.

No response.

Maybe one day, but not today.

Don't hope too much, Ella.

She returned to the noisy, crowded soup kitchen—and wondered how much more the church could do if corporations such as NHC had a vested interest in helping people like Freddie and Mavis.

Most of all, she wondered what J.D. would say. If she asked. Which she wouldn't. The less J.D. knew of her work, the less she'd need to keep from him.

J.D. lay a long time without moving, pretending to sleep.

God almighty, his father had come to visit him. He'd known the instant the old man sat down in the chair next to the bed. Pops had brought the smell of snow with him and a hint of the house of J.D.'s childhood, that light musty scent of aged hardwood floors and water leaks and decades of boots at the back door.

Truth was, long ago J.D. had loved the old house with its tiny, boxed rooms and gingerbread eaves and massive spruce on the thumbprint-sized front lawn.

Face it, J.D., you loved that house on Birch Avenue far better than your sleek condo in Manhattan. The condo half the size of his daddy's home and costing twenty years of the old man's pay.

With a long, slow breath, he opened his eyes and looked at the empty chair where his father had sat. Why hadn't he let the old man know he was awake? Why hadn't he said, *Hey, Pops. How you doing? Good to see you. It's been too long.*

Because J.D. didn't know how to connect with his father.

Was it any wonder he shied away from getting too serious in a relationship with a woman? Oh, he'd tried a couple of times to go the distance, but each time the relationship had ended. He hadn't been able to tell the woman he loved her. He hadn't needed, wanted, yearned the way he supposed a man should if he loved a woman. Without a qualm, he could put her out of his mind.

Ella Wilder was his doctor, his single link to the outside. He *had* to think of her. That would end tomorrow upon discharge. Once he got back to the Walnut River Inn and his laptop, he had no doubt the sweet-voiced doctor would be a distant memory.

Liar. You can't wait until she's back on shift so you can see her, talk to her. J.D. frowned. All right, he admitted she was easy on the eyes, but she could never be in his picture. She was small town; he'd become a city boy. She was family oriented—working with her brother was proof; J.D. was a loner. His gut crimped. *Your dad came to see you, jerk, and you pretended to be asleep. You don't have to be alone. It's what you choose.*

And there it was. Once again, he was listing reasons not to smell the roses—as the adage went. Yeah, he was a regular class act.

So why did he feel so damned disillusioned?

Because, had he opened his eyes, looked at his old man, they would have had nothing to say to each other.

Nothing at all.

Same as always.

Chapter Six

She wouldn't rush to his room first. She would do her rounds in order this time. No favorites.

But she couldn't wait to see him and wondered if he felt the same, if he had this crazy yearning to lock eyes, this need to hear her voice, her words. Was he waiting for her hands on his skin?

Don't miss me too much, okay?

Twenty-four hours, and he'd been right. She missed him, and it was…strange and thrilling. And when she rose at dawn, dressed, ate her bowl of oatmeal, excitement had run through her.

She tried not to glance out her kitchen window and across the alley to the house where J.D. had been raised. Yesterday afternoon when she'd called the nurses' desk to obtain a quick update on her patients, she'd been told of J.D.'s visitor. June had recognized the old man; after all, he had been in Ella's care four months ago, lying in the room across the hall from where J.D. was recovering.

"What's wrong with me, Molly?" she asked the cat twining around her ankles. "It's like I'm sex starved." At that she sighed. It wasn't possible to be sex starved when you'd never feasted at the banquet. *Jeez.* How was she coming up with this drivel?

"I won't deny it," she muttered, setting out a fresh bowl of water for Molly. "I've had *it* on the brain since *he* came into my care."

And then there were the dreams and fantasies. With J.D. naked and her naked and bed sheets and pillows and kisses and hands here and fingers there and…

Sheesh, Ella! Enough already!

Wishing she'd booked a two-week vacation and gone to California to visit her brother David, she slung on her coat, grabbed her keys and trudged out the back door.

A vacation would've prevented her from treating J. D. Sumner.

At 6:58 a.m. she began her rounds. First was a teenager with a broken shoulder, next was a seventy-year-old woman who'd need spinal surgery. Ella worked down the list, deliberately slowing her pace as she treated her patients, conscious the distance to J.D.'s room shrunk with each step.

And then he was next. "Good morning," she sang, sailing through the open doorway.

He lay on his side facing her. Ashley, the physiotherapist, worked J.D.'s leg.

"It's not *that* good," he grumbled through white lips.

"Problems?" Ella asked the woman.

J.D. answered, "I'm out of here, Doc, whether you say so or not. I'm not staying another day."

She stood beside Ashley, who paused the exercise so Ella could see the area of concern. "Looks fine. The swelling is gone, the incision is healing nicely." She checked his heart rate for ten seconds. "Pulse is normal. Good circulation." Scanning his chart, she saw his BP reading an hour ago was one-ten over seventy. Excellent. "All right," she said. "You can go any time after eleven."

"Why not now?"

"Because," she said as Ashley gathered her tools and left the room, "I instruct my patients with home care before they leave."

J.D. frowned. "So do it now."

"I don't have time now." She moved toward the door.

"Then later. I'll call you from the inn."

"Won't you be staying with your father?"

His eyes narrowed. "News does travel fast."

She gave him an encouraging smile, but he looked away. "I won't be staying with him," he said.

Something in his tone, the turn of his mouth, had her returning to the bed. "Is everything okay, J.D.?"

He drew a hard breath. "As to be expected." Cynicism flicked across his eyes. "My father and I aren't on the best of terms. That okay enough for you?"

For several seconds she studied him. "Want to talk about it?"

His lips lifted imperceptibly. "You my confessor now, Doc?"

"We can be good sounding boards if necessary."

"Doctor-patient confidentiality and all that?"

"Exclusively."

He pinched the bridge of his nose. "Look. Pops and I haven't talked in, I don't know, five years or more. We're not the communicative kind. He does his thing, I do mine. Why he came yesterday is beyond me. I didn't call him or ask him to come."

"You're his son," she said simply.

He stared. "You're kidding, right?"

"Not at all. Fathers are funny. They may not seem like they care, but most often it's that they care too much." She thought of her own dad, whom she missed more than she could describe. What she wouldn't give to have one more minute—heck, thirty more seconds with him. J.D. was luckier than he realized.

"Caring wasn't on my old man's agenda," he said. "Pops couldn't wait for me to leave home. Know what he said when I turned eighteen? 'If you're gonna get a life, get a damned good one. End of story.' He loved staying that. 'End of story.'" With an abrupt grin the darkness left his eyes. "There you go, Doc. Got some jeez for my whine?"

Ella couldn't help laughing. "Okay—jeez," she repeated, glad to see that sexy smile again. "And for your effort I'll drive you back to the inn." She strode for the door.

"Wait a sec," he called before she could escape. "You don't drop an offer like that and go."

Ella paused in the doorway. "Our policy is we don't leave our patients stranded."

"That's going a bit above and beyond, isn't it?" His eyes bored into hers. "What's in it for you?"

"In it for me?" For a moment, she stared at him before realizing he saw it as some kind of payoff. Anger struck. "There is nothing in it for me, Mr. Sumner. Our hospital may not have everything your company can offer, but there is one thing we do have and that's heart. Our doctors and nurses care for our patients, not just in here, but when they leave the premises. We want them to heal, which means following their treatment to the end. We don't want them back here."

His eyes softened. "Okay," he said. "You've convinced me."

"I'll see you at eleven."

"Ella."

Again, she waited.

"I'm glad you're my doctor," he said quietly.

She did not return his smile. Nodding once, she left. What on earth had she gotten herself into?

Oh, Ella, you are in such deep, deep water with this man.

For the first time in twenty years, she had no idea how to swim.

Stomach in a knot—which she blamed on too much caffeine—she returned to his room at eleven. It was empty, tidy, the bed linens changed and pulled to military standards. His cell phone, water bottle, watch—all that was his—were gone from the night table. She turned and went to the nurses' station.

"Mr. Sumner check out, June?" she asked the nurse sitting at one of the computers.

"He left about ten minutes ago."

"Did someone pick him up?"

"Not that I saw. He told us he was leaving and that he'd catch a cab. Didi assisted him downstairs. She was taking her lunch break afterward so you'll probably find her in the cafeteria."

"Thank you." Ella took the stairs to the main floor.

Between a pair of crutches, J.D. stood at the big windows beside the entrance doors with Didi at his side. Both looked toward the access lane and parking lot where people, bundled in winter wear, came and went.

"You were supposed to wait," Ella murmured coming to stand beside J.D.

"Hey, Dr. Wilder," Didi greeted from J.D.'s other side. "Cab shouldn't be much longer."

"Thanks, Didi. Go have your lunch. I'll wait with Mr. Sumner."

The nurse nodded, understanding Ella's need to have a moment with her patient. She handed over a plastic sack.

When they were alone, Ella gazed out at the gray day. This morning's skiff covered most vehicles' hoods and roofs. A taxi drove up and stopped in front of the doors and a nurse waiting with an elderly woman using a walker hurried out to speak to the driver. Seconds later, the woman eased her patient into the front seat, then climbed into the rear and the cab drove away.

"That standard around here?" J.D. asked. "Medical staff taking patients home?"

"Only if the patient has no family or someone to pick them up. We don't put people in cabs and say *sayonara* after having surgery. Too much can go wrong. A nurse will ensure the patient is secure and comfortable in their home before leaving the premises."

"Are these special nurses you've hired for the job?"

"They're home-care nurses who work out of the hospital."

"You going to tuck me into my room?"

No, but I want to. Shoving the thought aside, she jingled the sack Didi had given over. "These your things?"

"Yeah. The rest are at the Walnut River Inn." He hobbled forward. "Changed my mind, Doc. I decided on a cab after all."

"And I told you I needed to give you some home-care instruction, then I'd drive you to where you wanted to go."

"Don't you have patients to cut into?"

"Not until this afternoon. It's my lunch break now and I take that at home when I can. Today I can."

An eyebrow lifted. "You want to take me to *your* home? Hell, why didn't you say? I would've waited in your car."

Just like that tension rolled from her shoulders. Her lips twitched. "You never miss a beat, do you?"

"Not when I can pull a smile from you."

Briefly, those green eyes between their pitch lashes

flashed and held her hypnotized. Mentally, she shook free. *Duty, Ella.* "My car is in the staff lot behind the hospital."

"Cab company's not going to appreciate losing a fare," he said and maneuvered his crutches around.

"There are always people needing rides from here," she said. "He'll earn his dollar, don't worry."

They walked slowly down the hallway leading to the rear of the building. When they'd reached the exit, she said, "I'll bring the car up so you don't have to go through the snow," then ran across the parking lot. While the motor warmed, she brushed off the thin coat of snow. Two minutes later, her Yaris sat parked beside the door and she hurried into the building.

"I'm not a complete invalid, Doc," J.D. muttered as she took his arm and assisted him to the passenger door.

"It's a safety measure. I don't want anything happening to that knee ever again."

"What about me?"

"What about you?" They'd reached the car and she lifted his right leg carefully as he positioned himself onto the seat.

This close she saw he'd missed a tiny spot shaving, right next to his ear lobe. Had he been in a hurry? Anxious to leave? Anxious about her offer to drop him at the hotel?

The scent of the hospital's soap on his skin shot pheromones into her veins.

"You're staring, Doc," he whispered.

Ella jerked back, bumping her head on the rim of the door.

J.D. winced, caught her hand. "Hurt?"

"A little. My fault."

He grinned. "Nah, it's mine. I have that effect on—"

She slammed the door shut. The man was impossible. And she was crazy to be taking him back to his room when Didi could have done the job as well.

She rounded the car, climbed behind the wheel.

"You okay?" he asked as she drove down the lane to a side street.

"Just peachy."

He shot her a grin. "A little touchy after the bump, are we?"

"Not at all. Hardly felt it."

At that he grunted. She drove through town. The snowplow had cleared most of the main arteries to the hospital and other public-service venues. Turning north, Ella headed down the long winding street toward the Walnut River Inn.

The B and B–styled hotel was one of Walnut River's first notable structures dating back to 1850 and located on a wooded acre fringing the town's outskirts. Through barren branches of ancient maples fronting the white clapboard three-story, a wide front porch with cane-backed rockers currently covered against winter, welcomed guests and visitors.

She pulled up along the curb near a wrought-iron street lamp advertising the inn's name. While she knew of the Inn, Ella had never ventured inside or met the owners.

J.D. gazed up the curved swept walkway sprinkled with sand. "It'll be damned good to eat a home-cooked meal again," he remarked. "All right. I'm out of here." He swung open the door.

"Hang on." Ella was out of the car and at his side in seconds.

"I can manage, Doc. I had knee surgery, not an amputation. At least not the last time I looked."

"Smart aleck," she said, handing him the crutches.

"How long do I have to use these?"

"A day or two, then I'd like you to use a cane." She took his arm. "For a few more days, until you can stand on the leg without pain. Ashley has booked you into PT for the rest of this week. Do you know where it's located?"

"Main floor. Opposite the library and solarium."

Slowly they went up the walk. "Next week you can attend the clinic across the street from the hospital. Keep with the antibiotics for seven days. Then I want to see you again." They had reached the Inn's front door.

J.D. held her in place, his long, hard fingers covering hers on his arm. "And I want to see you again, Ella."

Her name in that deep voice caught her breath. "I've sched—"

"I mean personally. Outside the hospital and my medical care."

She shook her head. "As I've said before, you're a patient."

Several heartbeats passed. He said, "We'll talk in a couple days. When I come to observe you and your floor."

Apprehension skipped up her spine; she recalled Peter's words about Henry Weisfield cutting deals with Northeastern HealthCare. "Just so you know, I'm not in favor of Mr. Weisfield's decision."

"Even if it meant a new CAT or bone-density scanner?"

"Ours work fine, J.D." She had to stand behind Peter, who knew more about the situation than Ella. As temporary chief of staff, Peter had an excellent finger on the budget pulse and the hospital's necessities.

"But new ones would be nice." His smile went into his eyes and she relaxed. Perhaps the company's agenda was only to assist small hospitals, not take them over. Perhaps she and Peter and everyone else had read their intentions wrong….

No. She couldn't lose sight of J.D.'s reason for being in Walnut River in the first place. Or NHC's takeover bid.

"Of course. State-of-the-art equipment is always on a hospital's wish list," she said smoothly, "but that doesn't mean we need to throw out our current equipment if it gives the data we require. That's excessive spending."

A cold wind whipped around the corner of the porch and cut through her jacket. They'd stood outside too long. Not wanting him to get cold, she pushed open the front door.

Immediately, the smell of baking had her stomach grumbling.

J.D. chuckled. "Greta's afternoon cookies. Come back at four when she sets a plate out in the parlor for the guests and I guarantee you'll be drooling like Pavlov's dog."

"I've never drooled," Ella replied, though her stomach rebelled. And she wouldn't be back here. At all.

J.D. leaned in close. "Oh, come on. Not even in high school when the class jock walked by?"

She snorted. "Especially not when he walked by. If your room is on another floor, I hope this place has an elevator."

"It's on the main." He bounced his eyebrows. "We could order in and have a quiet lunch together."

"I'll pass. I need to feed my cat. Take care, J.D." Now that she was leaving and wouldn't be seeing him again, except once more for a checkup, sadness slipped into her heart. He was a good man who made her laugh when most of her days were serious.

On impulse, she hugged him, meaning it to be quick and sisterly. But his left arm closed around her and held her against his body for several beats longer than appropriate.

Oh, but he felt wonderful, all hard angles and long, lean bones and with her nose pressed against his jacket, his scent filled her lungs. Her heart trembled. Had he kissed her hair?

"I'll miss you," he said, voice sandy.

She stepped from the warmth of his clasp. "Bye."

Outside, she welcomed the biting wind on her hot cheeks.

He's your patient, Ella. There are ethics involved, don't forget.

Never mind that he worked for the wrong company.

Thirty minutes later, J.D. sat on his bed and opened the chicken sandwich he'd had delivered from Prudy's Menu. Greta, the Inn's owner, had recommended the place for the best sandwiches in town. Prudy. Jeez, she'd brought him home-baked cookies from her shop when he was a kid. Some things never changed.

And some things had. They were changing whether he liked it or not. His dad's silent visit, for example. What had it meant? The old man never went out of his way to see J.D., to communicate. But the minute he got laid up, Pops appeared like a shadow on the wall.

Then there was Dr. Ella. When had a woman consumed his mind the way she did? All she had to do was walk past him and he wanted to take her to bed. And that hug in the foyer? He'd damn near sunk his tongue into the wet warmth of her mouth. Damn near dragged her into the bedroom, slammed the door and sunk into her other parts.

His heart thudded in his chest, his groin pulsed to the beat. The woman was driving him crazy. He wished to hell NHC hadn't demanded he tour the hospital for the next week or so. He wished he could avoid physiotherapy tomorrow.

He did not want to see her again.

He couldn't wait to see her again.

The sandwich sat on the night table, forgotten. Was she back at the hospital, treating her patients? Was she preparing for surgery, going over vitals, charts, records, asking questions? Was the patient young, old, male, female?

He envied the person hearing her voice, feeling the warm, gentle touch of her hands.

J.D. scrubbed his palms down his cheeks. He was a jerk. Those patients were in pain, otherwise they wouldn't be having surgery. How could he envy that?

Because you're letting a woman control your emotions.

At that he almost laughed. "Like you have any

emotions *to* control," he muttered. Popping a painkiller, he realized a truth. Ella Wilder had cracked the corroded lock on his heart.

Two days and she hadn't seen him, not on the main floor, heading for physio, not wandering the second floor on an "observation" hunt for his employer.

What had she expected?

Nothing. He was a patient, one leaving Walnut River in a couple of weeks. Then why on earth had she expected...*something*? She asked herself the question again while standing at the big stainless steel sinks and scrubbing for the arthroscopy she would perform on a forty-year-old woman experiencing early signs of arthritis.

You need a life, Ella. You need to go to a bar, have a couple of margaritas, sit beside some hunk on a stool and let the cards fall where they will. Or go shopping, buy a bikini and fly to some beach where sweaty guys played volleyball in the sand. Any of the above won't lead to expectations. They'll lead to...to...

Sex. Plain and simple.

Sex without conditions.

Sex without commitment.

Sex, sex, sex.

"Patient is ready, Doctor," the circulating nurse called from the O.R. doorway.

"Be right there, Shelly."

Get your mind on task, Ella, or you're going to regret ever meeting J. D. Sumner. You are not a sex-starved woman. You are a doctor. Breathing deep, she stepped away from the tub. *Okay. Count backward. Ten, nine, eight, seven... All right. You're good to go.*

Water dripping, she walked to the hot-air dryer, punched it on with an elbow. Keeping her hands aloft, she pushed butt first through the doors of the O.R. where the scrub nurse tugged a pair of surgical gloves over Ella's fingers. She pushed back the flutter of nerves as she surveyed the instruments placed on the stainless steel trays. "How's Wanda doing?" she asked the anesthesiologist.

"Out."

"All right. Let's make her a new knee."

Two hours later, surgery complete, Ella headed for her examination offices on the fourth floor. Rounding the corner of the corridor leading to the bank of elevators, she gasped when a big body blocked her way and a hand gripped her arm. "J.D.!"

"Hey, Doc, where's the fire?"

The crutches were gone, the cane in place—which he leaned on while he released her slowly, amusement in his eyes. Navy flannel pants outlined the contours of the knee brace and a gray sweater contoured his impressive shoulders.

She brushed at her bangs. "What are you doing here?"

"Working on my report."

Ella's mind blanked when she caught sight of his full bottom lip. His mouth hitched; her gaze shot up. Green eyes glinted.

"Sorry I can't chat," she said, feeling abashment creep along her neck. "I have patients waiting."

"What about this patient?"

She headed down the hall. "You're healing very fast, I see." He followed with barely a limp.

"Have dinner with me, Ella."

She had no time for this. "Are you asking because I'm your doctor and you want information about the hospital?"

He scowled. "I'm asking because I like you. Because—as I've said before—I'm attracted to you."

"Which is why we can't have dinner." Darn, the elevator car was stopping at every floor. She should have taken the stairs. "I don't date patients."

"First, no offense, but I've switched doctors. I have an appointment with Dr. Taggart in Pittsfield for my follow-ups. Second, I'm staying till the end of the month. I've decided to take vacation time after my assignment with WRG is finished."

Panic. Excitement. She squelched both. "J.D., this is not—"

"Please, Ella."

The *please* streamed through her, warm as melted chocolate.

Ding. The car had arrived, the doors slid open. She stepped inside, turned.

He stood with both hands stacked on the handle of the cane, his expression as serious as she'd ever seen. "Will you?"

The doors began to close. "All right," she said quickly. Before the door shut him out, before she could analyze her response.

"Tonight," he called. "I'll call you."

And then she was alone.

She leaned against the wall, hung her head.

Lord. Her brain cells went AWOL when it came to J. D. Sumner. The man was her patient. *Had been* her patient—an act he'd accomplished with deliberate purpose, she was certain. Worse, he worked for a company proposing to take over her hospital.

Don't let Peter find out about J.D.'s personal intentions, was all she could think.

Chapter Seven

Standing in her kitchen, cuddling Molly into her neck and stroking the cat's satiny head, Ella listened to J.D. on the answering machine. He wanted her to call him at the Inn.

Again, she hit Play. Again, his deep voice traveled along the nerves under her skin. If she closed her eyes and imagined…

He stood right behind her, his arms wound around her waist, his hands were on her breasts—

She blinked against the bright kitchen lights. *Fool!*

Setting the cat on the floor, she decided to phone and renege with some excuse. She couldn't *not* call him.

He picked up on the second ring. "I'm sorry, J.D.," she said without preliminaries. "But I can't make dinner tonight. I just got in and I need to go over some notes. I have an early morning meeting."

"It's only dinner, Ella. Not the entire night. Much as I'd like it to be."

She sighed. "I've never met a more persistent man."

"Good. How long will it take you to get here?"

She glanced at the clock. 6:45 p.m. "Half hour." She replaced the receiver before he could respond.

Naturally, he phoned back. "Yes?"

"You pick the place, but make it somewhere nice. And wear a dress." The phone buzzed in her ear.

She looked at Molly, hobbling away, tail flicking the air as if to say, *Fine. Go with him. Don't think of me being home alone.*

Ella swooped up the cat and hurried down the hall. "Oh, Mol." She kissed the animal's head. "You're my special someone."

In the bedroom, she dropped the cat on the quilt and turned for the closet. Forty minutes later, dressed in a brown skirt and an ochre sweater, she was late, excited and nervous. And she gloried in the emotions. It had been so long, so very long since a man had her head in a tizzy and her blood humming.

He stood waiting under the Inn's mellow porch light.

Oh my oh my, but he was beautifully male. Ten years she had examined people, living and deceased, and none had appeared as fit and hale and rugged as J.D. standing on that porch in the semi-darkness of winter. Tall and elegantly dressed in black boots and a long black trench coat, he conveyed a blend of sophistication and danger.

"Where is your cane?" she asked, coming up the walkway.

"Don't need it." He waited until she stood on the bottom step. "I have you." And then he smiled.

If the words *I have you* hadn't sent her to the ground in a puddle, the smile had her gripping the newel post for support.

Soon, she thought. *You will have me. If you wish.* And she saw by his eyes that he did wish…very much.

She went up the stairs, latched onto his arm to assist him down the snowy walkway.

"You are definitely irredeemable, Mr. Sumner. And brash. And, I suspect, unrepentant."

He chortled. "How are you, Doc? By the way, you look fantastic in a skirt. Nice change from those scrubs. Not that I don't like the scrubs, but I don't get to see your lovely legs in them."

Her stomach did a slow twirl. "If you must know, I didn't have time to shave them. Just saying." The non-shave had been deliberate, done to prevent her from doing anything too risqué. Like undressing for him.

"Shaved legs are overrated."

Scoffing mildly, she started them toward the car. "You wouldn't say that if you saw me—" *Naked.*

"Without any clothes?" His eyes were ripe with humor. "Good. Can't wait to get whisker burn."

Her blood went thick. "Hmph."

As she had done three days before, she assisted him into her car. Tonight, however, she did not look into his eyes or pause to sniff the scent on his clothes and hair. Rather, she tucked in his wounded leg and closed the door.

Behind the wheel, she said, "If you don't mind, I'd like to eat in Pittsfield. There's an excellent restaurant called the Dakota that serves the best steaks and seafood you've ever eaten."

"I know the place," he said.

Yes, she thought. Walnut River was his childhood home after all. She pulled from the curb.

They headed out of town and, within minutes, were on the highway leading west. In the CD player Jann Arden sang her poignant *Greatest Hurts*. For the next ten minutes Ella couldn't think of a thing to say—but, oy—she could feel him sitting a foot away, big and invincible, crowding the dash-illuminated confines of her little car. The light swiped the blade of his nose, the perimeter of his cheekbones, the camber of his lips. And whenever he turned his head she felt his glance sear into her flesh. She flicked off the vents, aching for a cold wind.

At last they reached the restaurant and she stepped from the car into the wintry night, relieved to be free of the silence and tension that had increased with every mile.

J.D. waited at the curb until she'd hooked her arm through his and they went inside the rustic restaurant with its hunting-cabin decor of canoes and elk and moose heads mounted from rafters and walls. In a cozy booth they sat across from each other and, under the soft shine of a wall lamp, scanned the menu. Ella ordered the wood-grilled chicken, no rice, extra vegetables, J.D. the filet mignon, medium rare. Neither ordered alcohol. She was the designated driver and he had a week's worth of antibiotics to finish.

After ordering, Ella looked at J.D. An edge of his mouth lifted in a quiet smile. "You haven't said more than ten words since we drove out of town," he said.

"I was thinking."

"About?" Intensity darkened his eyes.

Her shoulders sagged a little. "Too much, I'm afraid."

"Things at work?"

She shook her head slowly, her eyes on his face. "Me." *You.*

For a moment he watched her. "I think about you, too. A lot. Maybe too much." He reached across the table. "Let me hold your hands, Ella."

"Why?" To the outsider the gesture would appear as if they were in a relationship. As if they were lovers.

"I'm betting they're cold."

She had the urge to take her clenched hands from her lap and shove them under her thighs for warmth, to hide. *Juvenile behavior.*

"Come on," he coaxed. "We're in Pittsfield. The likelihood of someone recognizing us is remote. That's why we're here, isn't it?"

Oh, she was in trouble. The man understood her far too well. "My hands are chapped," she said swerving from his implication that she wanted to keep their outing a secret. "Too many scrubbings."

"They're the gentlest, most beautiful hands I've seen. They can hold a scalpel and scrape an eyelash off a gnat, they're so steady." Smiling, he held out his palms. "Let me, Ella."

She hadn't gotten past "most beautiful." He was too charming, too magnetic. Entranced, she slid her hands over the wooden surface of the table and he curled his fingers around her, warm as a flame.

"You're like ice." And then he bent his head over their joined hands, blowing a soft gust of air against her fingers, his mouth brushing her thumbs.

Oh, my. Such a simple, sensual act and with a thousand tingling responses!

"J.D.," she whispered, amazed her voice still worked.

"Don't be nervous. It's just me."

"*That's* the problem."

He peered up; stroked his thumbs over the surface of her hands. "What am I going to do with you, Doc?" he asked, though she felt the question was more a self-analysis. Straightening, he set her free. "You are a puzzle. I can't figure you out. Do you know this is a first?"

"What is?" Back in her lap her fingers slid into the opposite sleeves of her light-knit sweater, sealing in the warmth from his body.

"That a woman has my head in a mess."

She forced a laugh. "Once you're back in New York your head will be fine. You'll be back to work, doing activities you're accustomed to." *Dating women who won't muddle your brain.*

"Have you ever thought of working in a bigger hospital?"

"Not once." Before she could explain, the waitress arrived with the bottles of sparkling water they had ordered, and when they were alone again Ella said, "I obtained my degree at Harvard and did my residency at Mass General. But I've always wanted to return home, back to Walnut River General. It's where I grew up and first learned about medicine. I owe that place my life." Smiling, she cupped her water glass. "My dad loved that hospital. He was a good and kind man and he taught me that medicine is an art defined by caring."

As she spoke, J.D. drew closer, setting an elbow on the edge of the table and propping a fist on his thigh.

"Sorry," she said, suddenly conscious of his scrutiny. "I tend to get on a bandwagon sometimes. What about you? What got you into health care?"

He leaned back, as if her question meant nothing, except his posture told a different story and a mask fell across his face. "I grew up believing hospitals weren't good or kind." He frowned and she sensed memories warred within his mind.

He went on. "My dad had a bad experience long ago. My mother died in childbirth." His eyes hardened. "Mine."

"Oh, J.D.... I don't know what to say. Your father must have suffered deeply." *And J.D.*, she thought. Subconsciously, he would have suffered a loss no child should ever experience—that abiding, nurturing love only a mother could give. Then, remembering Prudy at Jared's bedside last fall, Ella took a chance. "Did he ever remarry?"

"Nope. Been a widower for thirty-six years."

That made the situation seem sadder. She imagined the little boy J.D. had been so long ago without a mother to come home to, without a mother to hear humming somewhere in the house—the way it had been with Ella's mother baking cookies. And her sweet-scented hugs. Alice had grown jasmine in her flower-beds and placed sachets among her clothes. It was the thing Ella recalled best, that lovely, light scent on her mother's skin.

Indeed, J.D. had missed a great deal.

The waitress arrived with steaming plates of chicken and filet mignon, fresh salads and seasonal vegetables. Suddenly, Ella realized she hadn't eaten since eleven-thirty that morning.

"Bon appetit," J.D. said with a wink.

For several moments they savored their meals. She was grateful he had suggested dining out; barring hospital food, she hadn't eaten a prepared meal since last summer. Which said something about her personal life. It didn't exist. *One day, Ella, you'll wake up an old maid facing menopause.*

The notion burned in her throat; she reached for her glass of water. Caught in the lamplight, fire stroked J.D.'s hair. From the moment she'd seen him in the E.R., that dark auburn color had attracted her. A color unusual on a man, yet on J.D., it pronounced his knife-keen cheek-bones and square jaw, his dark brows.

Black lashes lifting, his eyes immobilized her across the table. Her every cell stood alert, sensitized.

"Dollar for your thoughts," he said in that deep, raspy Sam Elliot voice.

"I love the color of your hair. I'd give my left kidney for it. Well, not really—" she sipped her water "—but I'd give it some serious consideration. Who'd you inherit it from, your dad or your mom?"

"My mother."

"She must have been very beautiful."

"My dad thought so."

"And you?"

"I concur. From the photos I've seen."

"I'm sorry you never got to know her, J.D."

A nonchalant shrug. "You don't miss what you don't know."

Ella disagreed. She suspected he had missed a mother's love far more than he would acknowledge. "I'll miss my parents forever. They were a very big part of my life." She could not imagine growing up without a mother—or a father, for that matter.

A rueful smile touched J.D.'s mouth. "You were lucky."

"I was," she admitted. "My mom used to read us bedtime stories when we were little, and my dad would come in and tickle our toes. Of course, that would get us all excited, and then we wouldn't want to go to bed at all. Mom would fuss and fume at my dad, but she'd be laughing while she shook her finger at him."

J.D. cut into his steak. "Pops wasn't a story reader. Never had the time." At Ella's frown he shrugged. "No big deal. Besides, he always said he'd read to me later. Good thing I learned to like reading on my own."

An awkward pause descended. Ella wanted his grin, his sexy grin, back, but the way he tilted his head, the relentless line of his mouth... A long-forgotten memory played across her mind.

She said, "I think you and I knew each other when I was a little girl. Well, not really knew each other…" She waggled her head. "Sort of were *aware* of each other."

As she hoped, J.D. laughed. "Now you're making stuff up." He lifted a forkful of mashed potatoes to his mouth.

"Actually, no." Pushing a lock of hair behind one ear, Ella shot him a grin. "My grandmother lived across the alley from your dad. Mom took my sister and me to visit once a week. The year I was in first grade, I saw a red-haired boy—" her gaze skimmed his hair again "—practicing on a skateboard down the cement walkway in Jared's back yard. Grandma said the boy had just gotten the board the day before. Anyway, it was summertime and I remember being fascinated by that skateboard and how the boy could ride like a pro. Then he started practicing in the back alley and I went to the gate and watched through the wooden slats for a long time."

He sat back on the bench. "Unbelievable."

"It is, considering I'd forgotten it myself until just now." Ella took a bite of chicken.

His smile was slow, striking. "So, Doc, we have a history."

A giggle she couldn't hold erupted. "I was six, J.D. Your skateboarding techniques and claim to fame lasted all of fifteen minutes at most before I got bored and went inside."

"Uh-uh, you can't reinvent the story here. You said you were fascinated, not bored."

"I take the fifth. We're talking a six-year-old's attention span."

He cut another piece of steak, dipped it into the extra gravy he'd ordered. "I was your first boyfriend."

"You were no such thing," she retorted.

"You remembered my red hair."

"Who wouldn't? In the sun it blazed like fire."

Whimsy danced over his features. "Like fire, huh?"

"Oh, for heaven's sake," she sputtered. "It's an analogy."

"I know what it is, Doc. I'm just pointing out that you've had me in your memory banks most of your life. Which means—"

"Absolutely nothing."

"—that I was your first boyfriend."

Laughing, she shook her head and pushed her fork into the final piece of chicken. "All depends on whose point of view."

"All right." He set his cutlery on his plate, pushed it aside. "How about this? While I'm in town I'm your boyfriend. Or if that's too tweenish, your significant other."

She studied his eyes, saw a glimmer of something deeper and more substantial.

"J.D.—"

The waitress interrupted to take their plates. J.D. ordered the seasonal fruit crisp for dessert. "One order, two spoons." His gaze was on Ella. "We're sharing tonight."

The words, the mood, *his look* pooled low and hot in her abdomen and she wondered if she'd ever breathe again. Then he looked around the room, said, "I like your style, Doc," and the spell was broken.

The discussion led to safer topics: his love of snowshoeing and hiking, her love of running. She surprised him by enjoying hard-hitting movies like *Blood Diamond*. Most women he knew, he told her, went for light comedies and chick flicks. Her taste in music varied, though she favored songs that spoke to the heart. And he surprised her by his preference for country music.

She ate only three bites of the crisp. Enough to let the sweetness alert her taste buds, and to have him dip his spoon in her area of the bowl, have metal click on metal while his expression specified he knew exactly what he was doing: sharing intimacies reserved for couples that were in each other's soul.

On the drive back to Walnut River, they spoke little, listening to a CD of twenty favorites from her collection at home. Roberta Flack's haunting voice about a woman seeing the face of a special man for the first time filled the dark interior. Although three decades old, the hit trembled through Ella in a way it hadn't before. It was as if the lyrics were hers, as if the singer saw J.D. through Ella's eyes.

She glanced across at the man in the next seat.

He had turned his head and his absorption was entirely on *her* face. Heart jamming her throat, she refocused on the headlights channeling the snow-shouldered highway.

"Just to let you know," he said quietly, "I'm going to kiss you when we get back to the Inn."

Heat shot through her. "Just to let *you* know, that will be my decision to make."

"Agreed. You can decide how hot it'll be."

She clenched the steering wheel to keep from driving off the road. "What if I don't want you to kiss me?"

"You do." His voice was soft sand, the tropical kind that burned your bare toes.

"You're awful sure of yourself." But she heard a quiver of excitement in her voice. She toughened her resolve. "Not every woman you meet wants to jump your bones, J.D."

"Nor do I. Want to jump the bones of every woman I meet."

She chuckled. "Wow. You have standards?"

He was silent for several miles. She drove through the winter darkness, aware her remark had ruined a lovely evening, shame replacing the heat his anticipated kiss had caused.

She stopped in front of the inn's sign, expecting him to throw open the door and climb out as fast as his injured knee would allow in order to get away from her and the chaos of their date.

Instead, he turned. "Yes," he said, threading a hand into the hair at her nape and tugging her gently across the console. "I do have standards. But you've broken them all."

And then he put his mouth on hers.

On initial contact she had thought he might be a devouring kind of guy but he surprised her yet again.

Soft, slow, tender. And everywhere she yearned for more and more and more.

She drank him; she inhaled him.

His fingers wove deeper into her hair, touched her face, trailed the line of her neck. Warm and flavored of fruit, his breath wisped her chin, whispered at her ears. Her eyelids fluttered shut and she rode the sensation, followed his lead, fell into his kiss—into *him*.

J.D. The thought emerged through the dizziness, the want, the need, like a bright, lone star at midnight.

Her hands found the fabric of his shirt, slipped upward along hard muscle and bone, crept around his neck. And hung on.

Was it a moment? She wanted forever.

At last, he lifted away, a finger's width. "Hello, Ella," he whispered and she felt his air caress her tender mouth.

"Hi," she whispered in return.

He kissed her again, a hint of lip to lip. "I need to go in," he said. "Before something…happens."

She didn't need to ask what. She was a doctor. She knew how a man's body functioned in passion. She knew how a woman's body responded and hers was already on fire, ready, willing to consume, *to be consumed*. Carefully, he eased back until he was on his side of the car again and their bodies no longer touched.

"I'll find my way in," he said.

She shook her head. "No, I don't want you slipping on the ice."

She got out to stand beside him on the sidewalk, gripping his arm. They walked to the porch, up the steps, to the door where she released him. "Good night, J.D.," she said. As if she hadn't had the lips kissed off her face two minutes ago.

"How long before you're home?"

"Ten minutes."

"I'll call then, make sure you're okay."

Under the light, she saw that his face held no humor. "I'll be fine, J.D. Thank you for a very enjoyable evening."

She trotted down the steps, strode for her car, welcoming the freezing night air against her swollen mouth, welcoming back wisdom and logic into her head. What she'd done in her little blue Yaris had neither wisdom nor logic, because she'd almost climbed into a man's lap and had sex for the first time and right in the middle of the street. She couldn't get home fast enough. She needed the shelter and safety of her house.

By the time she arrived and put the car in the garage, she was calmer, her body in sync to mind and emotion.

Until she opened the kitchen door and heard the phone playing its "Here Comes the Sun" ringtone.

Chapter Eight

J.D. listened to the fourth ring. She should've been in her house; she'd been gone fifteen minutes, five more than she'd estimated.

Sitting in his skivvies on the four-poster king-sized bed, he stared at the phone in his hand. What was the matter with him that he needed to know she was okay, that he needed to hear her voice again?

He moved to disconnect the cordless when he heard a faint "Hello?" and snatched the phone to his ear.

"You're home," he said unnecessarily.

"Sleep well, J.D."

"I had a great time tonight," he interjected before she clicked off. "I wanted to tell you, but you took off before I got a word out." *Argh*. He sounded like a petulant kid.

Silence. Then, "I'm on E.R. rotation this weekend, so late nights are not an option."

All right, he wouldn't quibble over two extra minutes. "When can I see you again?"

Tonight, he'd barely scraped the surface of Ella Wilder, but what he saw under those meager scuffs beckoned him like a starved man. He didn't understand why he felt the way he did. What he knew was that he'd been empty, heart and soul, for years, maybe all his life and Ella...Ella was a pool of warm water filling up a deep and parched well.

Jeez, why not write some painful teenage poetry, J.D.? I'm sure that *would impress her.* He gave himself a mental shake.

"—and a very busy week ahead," she was saying.

He'd missed half her conversation with all his mooning. "How about coffee then? At the hospital? Ten minutes—"

"Don't you have reports to write? An agenda to meet for NHC?"

"I do, but I also take breaks. Listen," he said, feeling her pull away as if tonight had never happened. "I was serious when I said I'll be your man while I'm in town. We can have a little fun—"

"And I'll be your woman so you get the info you need? That about right?" Her tone was cooler than he'd yet heard.

"Work won't enter the picture. Unless you want it to. Deal?" He scraped at his hair, waiting for her response. When it didn't come he said, "Ella, I just want to see you again. That's it. No hidden agenda. I like you. More than I want to admit, even to myself. You bewitch me. God knows why. I mean I do know why. You're gorgeous, intelligent, witty, sophisticated. Hell." Again a frustrated hand pawed through his hair. "I've never had this happen before."

"This," she said and her voice had softened. "As in wanting a relationship with someone you don't want a relationship with?"

"Yeah. No. Sort of. It's difficult to explain. That kiss tonight…Look, short of sounding like a teenage jock, you do something to me."

The line went quiet. God, he'd offended her with all his idiotic rhetoric. Phone still attached to his ear, he lifted his aching leg onto the bed, sank against the pillows. "Ella?"

"You do something to me, too," came her whisper.

Tiredly, he closed his eyes. "Thank you."

"We'll talk later. Meantime, go visit your father, J.D. He needs you." And then she hung up.

Exhaling slowly, he pressed End. Ten minutes—or was it longer?—he stared at the ceiling with its intricate scrolls and swirls.

She had known of their family since she was six, when J.D. hadn't known a thing about hers until a week ago. Until he met her brother in a boardroom and Ella in the E.R., in the building where his mother had died, the building his dad had hated for more than three decades.

He needs you, she said, minutes ago.

And I need him. The thought startled J.D. For twenty years the bond between he and his old man had steadily eroded. *Not too late to remedy that while you're here.*

Who was he kidding? Pops wasn't a warm, fuzzy kind of guy. And neither was J.D. The old man wouldn't give a rat's ass if his son showed up on his doorstep. Hell, he'd probably tell J.D. he deserved a banged-up knee for not paying attention and slipping on those steps.

He came to see you in the hospital. And that was the crux of it. Old Jared had sought out his son, came to offer support not censure. He'd sat at the side of the bed, still as stone, not opening his mouth once. In those minutes, J.D. sensed a difference in his dad, an unfamiliar difference, one that bordered...heartbreak. Could it be?

Confused, he crawled under the covers.

He'd think about it in the morning, when daylight brought a clearer head and a better attitude.

Weekend rotations during the winter months were often crazy. The weather did not mix well with the townsfolk. They broke ankles, wrists, legs, fractured elbows, injured rotator cuffs, dislocated shoulders. Most injuries were the result of icy traffic accidents, winter sports, shoveling snowy roofs and walkways, disconnecting strings of Christmas lights.

This Saturday, Ella's waiting room was already packed when she read the chart of her first patient, Florence MacGregor, the elderly mother of West MacGregor, who managed the hospital's budget. Last October, when Ella operated on her hip, Florence had shown signs of Alzheimer's.

Now, entering the room with the set of recent X-rays she'd ordered from radiology, she saw the white-haired woman on the examination table, wringing her hands. "Hello, Florence," she greeted.

"Hi, Dr. Wilder. West—he's my son—he wants to talk to you after. He's in the…the…kitchen." Briefly her blue eyes went blank before memory returned. "He's in the waiting room."

Ella nodded. "I'll have a chat with him when we're done. Now, let's have a peek at those hips of yours." She shoved the first X-ray onto the light box. "Right hip looks fabulous, Florence. How's the physio going?"

"I like it," she said. "West is such a good boy. He takes me all the time and helps around the house. He doesn't mean to be overprotective. It's just that he's got so much on his plate, y'know?"

Ella smiled. She wished more children would be as concerned about their aging parents as West was about Florence. "Sometimes overprotection is a good thing."

"Mm-hm." Florence stared at the next X-ray Ella put up. "Does my hip need a…replace…replacement?"

Ella rolled her stool closer and took the old lady's gnarled hand. "We talked about this last fall, Florence. Remember? I wanted your right hip to heal completely before we did the left one."

"It hurts when I walk and…and…and…."

"I know," Ella said gently. "That's why I've scheduled you for surgery on May second. I'll tell West, okay?"

Florence bobbed her head. "West is a good boy. He doesn't want me to worry about the cars." A frown. "I mean the cooking."

"Nor should you," Ella said as though nothing was

amiss. Giving the woman's hand a gentle squeeze, she rose from the stool. "Now let's have a little peek at your new hip. Can you lie down for me?" Keeping her voice soft, she carefully assisted Florence into position.

Ten minutes later, Ella left her patient to dress, then instructed the nurse to send West to her office at the end of the hallway.

"You wanted to see me, Doctor?" a voice asked as she was updating Florence's file. West stood in the doorway of her tiny office. As always he wore a classy dark suit, and his thin face held no smile.

"Hi, West. Take a seat."

She summarized his mother's case. "Don't be alarmed if she's in the hospital longer this time. It'll be her second surgery in a little more than six months, which can set back healing a few weeks."

"Guess it's to be expected," he said. "She is seventy-five."

"Yes. However, there are seniors who've healed more rapidly, but generally those people have maintained a routine of exercise."

West bounced a knee. "And Mom hasn't."

"No. Last fall she admitted she hates exercising. Most people do, so she's not alone. That's why I'd like you to get her involved in a group exercise program along with her physio. Thirty minutes of gentle exercise four or five times a week will help a lot. For now."

"For now?"

Ella considered. The man was Florence's primary care-taker, as well as hospital staff. "I'll be frank, West. Last fall, I mentioned that your mother is heading into dementia. I know it's not an easy thing to hear about a parent, but I strongly urge you to have her tested. For your sake and hers. I know the name of a great doctor who would—"

"No, that's okay." West shook his head and stood. "I'll look into it. Thanks." Pausing at the door, he said, "By the way, that NHC fellow, J. D. Sumner? He's a patient of yours, right?"

Surprised at his turn of topic, Ella said, "You know I can't divulge that information."

"Sure. Just thought you should know he's asking people all kinds of questions. What certain floors need equipment-wise, what doctors want to see upgraded, that sort of thing. I'm wondering why he requires all that info."

A prickle ran up her spine. While she was aware of the situation, she didn't care for West's tone or conjecture. "I'm sure it's something he and the board have discussed," she said calmly, though her heart booted her ribs.

He shrugged. "Interesting, though, don't you think? He comes to town, and suddenly the hospital is notified by the state investigator's office of patients being charged transportation costs by the hospital because there's no one to pick them up after surgery. They've also claimed doctors keep patients longer than necessary. Meantime, this guy's tallying lists for NHC." Another shrug. "Hope Peter knows what he's doing, is all." Then he was gone.

Ella stared at the empty doorway. She knew Peter had been reviewing a notice from the state investigator's office the morning of J.D.'s surgery. But did it relate to her patient?

It doesn't, a small inner voice said.

Then why had West implied J.D. was behind these notifications? And…had her hormone overload around the man blinded her?

Peter sat on the board as temporary chief of staff. He would safeguard the hospital's interests.

She picked up her pen. *Focus on your patients. They come first.*

Still, the unpleasant niggle West had planted lurked in her mind for the remainder of her shift. After all, *she* had insisted J.D. stay in the hospital an extra day.

J.D. stood in the hospital library overlooking the snowy gardens Pops had landscaped a lifetime ago. He recalled his dad cussing about needing the money that came with prettying up the place where his young wife had met her fate. Thing was, when the gardens were that job, Grace was still alive and J.D. a mere twinkle in the old man's eye.

Right. As if the old man's eyes ever twinkled. Well, maybe they had once—around Grace.

This morning, when he'd showered and shaved, J.D. had a certain gleam in *his* eyes. He'd woken on the ebbing tide of an erotic dream about Ella.

He massaged the back of his neck. The woman was in his blood and he had to get her out. But how, dammit? How did you stop thinking, wondering, *feeling*? Feeling, for God's sake. When the hell had he wanted more than sex from a woman?

Bracing a hand on the window frame, he studied the

gardens and pictured his dad digging in the soil. Had he brought Grace around, showed her the result, his pride palpable? J.D. imagined her telling Jared, *I love what your hands have done.*

Your hands.

Last night at the Dakota, hadn't he said virtually the same words to Ella? Marveled at the skill of her nimble fingers?

She'd cut open a part of his body—something more intimate than anything he'd dealt with in bed—and healed him.

So where are you going with this, J.D.? What does the old man and his gardens have to do with your attraction to Ella? On the economic spectrum, never mind the intellectual one, they're ten thousand miles apart.

And so was he. She came from a family of doctors and he spawned from a family of dirt diggers. He had no business lusting after her, yet the thought of leaving her staggered him.

She would not leave this town or this hospital; she'd told him so last night, though heaven only knew why he'd broached the subject in the first place.

Which meant…what? That he should stay?

Would that be so bad? a rascal on his shoulder asked.

Hell, yes!

He had no intention of relocating. He had a career in New York. He had money in New York. Dozens of women. A kick-ass condo. Why the hell would he want to move back to Walnut River?

Because she's here. Because your old man is here.

Because you're thirty-six years old and when it comes right down to it, that condo, those women, that career won't visit you in the old folks home. And they sure as hell won't stand at your gravesite one day, mourning your loss. He wasn't fool enough to think it for a second.

So, where did that leave him?

Frustrated, he turned from the snowy gardens, and limped out of the library. There were several more people to interview for his business bulletin. At least in this he had a goal. He could do something worthwhile for the hospital.

And her.

Tired to the bone, Ella locked her office at 5:20 p.m. and headed for the elevator. She couldn't wait to get inside her little house, run a hot bath, cuddle in her flannel pajamas on the sofa with Molly and dig into some Chinese takeout. Healthy or not, greasy chicken dumplings sounded perfect as long as a stove and dishes weren't involved.

On the way down to the main floor, she wondered if J.D. liked takeout. *Good grief. You're barely done at work and he's on your mind again.*

In truth, he'd been in her mind since West MacGregor dumped that information two hours ago. The J.D. she'd come to know—yes, it had been only a week—made her laugh and feel and think about things outside her work. Above all, he tangled up her emotions. No man had done that before.

But did she *really* know him?

Last night he thought she could do better than Walnut River General. Had his questions meant NHC's plans were already in place for her hospital, and he would rather she wasn't here to experience them?

Somehow, the two didn't mesh. J.D. might be business through and through, but he wasn't a user. His interest in her was purely hormonal.

Are you sure?

No, dammit, she wasn't, but right this minute she was too tired to go through a long, weary analysis. One thing was certain, and her heart ached at the thought. If she was this confused, she needed to take a break from him.

Hurrying toward the rear exit and staff parking on the main floor, she caught sight of chestnut hair peeping above the back of a cushiony chair in the solarium at the end of the corridor. She'd recognize that color anywhere. Heart tripping, she approached the open doors. Except for J.D., the room was empty. Silently, she walked forward.

He was asleep.

A knot filled her throat. During his hospitalization she had not seen him so relaxed—or so vulnerable.

Carefully, she perched on the edge of an adjacent chair. His head had fallen slightly to the right; the lines between his black brows lay quiet, peaceful. The corners of his mouth were innocent as a napping toddler's—that mouth she had kissed, which had kissed her. With passion and tenderness.

She fancied herself leaning over him, setting her lips there again, waking him with nibbles and caresses and sighs. She imagined cupping his bristly cheeks, threading her fingers through that thick, lustrous hair that hooked the light from an end-table lamp.

A triangle of white cotton lay in the V of his navy sweater and the sight of that bit of cloth, that *masculinity*, sent a hot spear into her belly. From that tiny point her gaze traveled his body: big, strong hands linked loosely across his abdomen, tailored black slacks, the bent left knee, the stretched right leg, the expensive black boots. Then back the same long route, up to his square chin, his beautiful mouth…and his watchful green eyes.

That quick she was seized by a wave of hunger and desire.

Drawing a deep breath, she broke the spell. "You looked so peaceful, I didn't want to wake you."

"How long…?" His voice was gruff from sleep.

"Few minutes."

He tugged himself up into the chair, checked his watch. "Seems I lost an hour."

"Evidently, you needed it. How's the knee holding up?"

"Holding." A hint of a smile.

"Did you cab it here?"

"Why? Are you offering to drive me home again?"

"Actually, I came to talk about last night." Gathering courage, she glanced at her hands clasped between her knees, took another breath. "Last night was lovely. But," she raised her eyes, "we can't do it again. I mean, we can't go out again. Together. Your employer is a company that might take over this hospital. Therefore, our association would be a conflict of interest."

An unreadable element flickered in his eyes. "By

whose standards, Ella? Yours or the hospital's? Way I
see it, unless there's a legal aspect to all this, the hospital
and for damn sure my employer have no business dic-
tating who I *associate* with. Nor do they control your
social calendar. That leaves you and me. Getting back
to last night, you're right—it *was* great. And I want to
do it again."

"J.D.—"

"Don't say it." Moving to the edge of his chair, he
caught her hands and brought her forward so their faces
were a foot apart. "I can't explain it either, but I need to
see you. Why do you think I'm prowling the corridors of
this hospital?" Before she could respond, he continued.
"Yes, I'm here for my company, but it's more than that.
I'm seeing things I'm not familiar with, ways and techniques I know don't exist in larger centers anymore.
There's camaraderie among staff members, a dedication
toward patients. Doctors and nurses don't rush people to
heal. And—" his smile touched his eyes "—I like it. I
think if I make my case right, NHC could reduce some
of the administrative overhead and implement a stronger
front where care is crucial. In other words, enhance
Walnut River General's community base."

He jiggled their hands. "I've seen you work in that
community, Ella. I've *been* part of that work." His eyes
darkened. "You make me want to do better, to be a better
man. Give us a chance."

"But you're leaving soon," she said and her voice
squeaked. His words had opened her heart like a bloom in
springtime. He wasn't the ogre MacGregor had insinuated.

"Not for a couple of weeks. By then…who knows? New York isn't so far away. A seventy-five minute flight to Hartford and a thirty minute drive here." He flashed a grin. "For me."

"A long distance relationship?" She couldn't help her disappointment. The first time a man had her insides churning and he was asking her to live for weekends. She got to her feet. "I really need to go home." *To think*.

Gripping the chair's arms, he rose gingerly to tower over her. "Have you eaten?"

"I'm picking up a couple boxes of takeout."

"Chinese?" One dark brow slanted upward.

"Yes. And no," she said on a laugh. "You are not invited. I need to have an early night."

"Tomorrow, then?"

Tomorrow was Sunday and she was still on call. "Sorry."

"Monday?"

Too close, he stood too close with those sparkling eyes, that kissable mouth, the scent of him swirling around her head. "That's three days away. I don't know what I'll be doing then."

"Good. Pencil me in."

Exasperated, she gave in. "Fine. Monday night." She moved out of the nook of comfortable chairs and soft lamplight that sent shadows dancing across the ridges of his face.

"What would you like me to bring?" he called as she walked toward the exit.

"Just yourself. I'll cook."

"What?"

Over her shoulder she repeated, "I'll cook."

"No, I mean *what* will you cook?"

She paused. He stood where she'd left him, tall and lean, hands in the pockets of his trousers, his honed body archetypical of the genuine red-blooded American male.

"Are you allergic to something?"

"Only Demerol." His grin curled her toes. "No food. Just like to know what's on tap in your kitchen."

"At this point I haven't a clue. You'll need to wait, and be surprised." She strode through the doors, already counting the hours.

Chapter Nine

He was surprised.

Surprised to get her call after three days of silence.
Surprised she offered to pick him up at the inn after work.
And surprised where she was taking him for the meal she
promised to create.

Dark as it was at five-thirty, the energy-saving street
lamps provided enough clarity for J.D. to recognize the
neighborhood the moment Ella's car headed east to the resi-
dential area known to locals as "down by the river." River-
dale, an offshoot suburb near Walnut River established in
the forties by blue-collar workers living in shanties which,
in later years, had been renovated by their offspring.

Like J.D.'s father, who had inherited land and house
from *his* dad.

The moment she turned down the darkened back alley, he couldn't keep calm. Where the hell was she taking him? Had she planned to take him to his dad's house all along?

Rubbing damp palms on his cargo pants, he asked, "You playing a game with me, Doc?"

Her head turned. "Game?"

"What're we doing down by the river?"

"This is where I live, J.D. In my grandmother's house." Slowing, she hit a garage door opener clipped to the sun visor, then pulled into the garage, turned off the ignition and, briefcase in hand, stepped out of the car. "My grandmother left the house to my sister and me. It's my home."

She took his arm as they left the garage. "I haven't cleared the walkway today, so watch your step. Sometimes there are icy patches."

J.D. glanced through her barren trees toward his former home across the alleyway. Night enveloped the building. When was the last time he'd been inside? Five years? Six? He couldn't recall exactly; the stay had been short. One day and a night, before he left angry and disappointed he and the old man hadn't connected, *again*.

Inside her house, a gray, three-legged cat purred greetings and butted their legs.

Ella lifted the feline. "This is Molly. Not allergic?"

"Nope." Pets hadn't been a part of his childhood.

"Good." Without removing her burgundy jacket, Ella went into the kitchen to fill a pair of stainless steel bowls with water and refrigerated meat; she set the bowls on the floor beside the stove.

J.D. removed his boots on the mat by the door. Purposely leaving his coat on, he went to stand by the sink to gaze out the window at the house where he'd grown up. The kitchen was lit, a shadow passed by the curtained window. Pops?

"Who lives there?" he asked, needing to be sure.

Ella came beside him. Their arms bumped. "Don't you know?" Her head turned and he felt the heat of her gaze.

"Few years ago, it was still my dad."

He felt her shift toward the window. "When was the last time you talked to him, J.D.?"

"Too long."

A heavy silence fell. Behind them the cat ate her meal, in another room a clock tick-tocked away the minutes. To the right, the refrigerator droned softly.

She said, "If you need to talk…"

"I don't." The top of her head was level with his shoulder. Her hair shone sleek and dark. Cut to an inch below her jaw, the length swung like a mini-veil when she looked up at him.

She dipped her head and the veil shielded her profile. "I'm not trying to pry, J.D., but bottling this up isn't good for you."

Deliberately, he turned, backed against the counter, arms folded. "You playing shrink, Doc? 'Cause if you are, I'm out of here. I'm hellaciously attracted to you, but my old man is off-limits."

Sadness shaded her eyes. "We're not so different, you know. What you're doing with your dad, I'm doing with my sister. We barely talk and when we do, it's all superficial. We rarely get together anymore. She lives in

New York, I'm here and," a shrug, "life goes on. It breaks my heart."

"Were you close?"

"Very. She's a year older, but it was like we were twins conceived at the same moment. She was my best friend. My dad used to say we were 'old soul friends'."

"What happened between you?"

Ella shrugged. "Things fell apart in college. I've never been able to figure out why, exactly. I think when she couldn't stand the blood and guts of medicine, she felt guilty. Here she was, part of a family of doctors and not able to *be* one. I think it affected her confidence. Which is stupid to the outsider, but not to the person it's happening to." She sighed. "I miss our friendship."

J.D. stared for a moment at the floor. "You were lucky to have that kind of relationship. The old man and I…" He huffed a laugh, pushed from the counter. "I don't want to talk about it." A half smile. "I know what you're doing, Doc. It isn't going to work."

She frowned. "Excuse me?"

"You share, then I share, that sort of thing?"

Her eyes flashed. "You think I told you about my sister to get you to talk about your family?" She walked across the kitchen, flung around. "I told you about her because I *wanted* to, J.D. Not because I thought you'd feel obligated to disclose your family history. I thought we had something here, at least that's what you keep insisting. Two days ago you were jumping all over a long-distance relationship. Seems I misinterpreted *long distance*. You meant emotions, not miles." Pulling out her keys, she headed for the back door. "Know what? I don't feel like cooking after all. I'll take you back to the hotel."

He was in front of her in three long strides, biting back the sharp sting in his knee. "Look, I'm sorry, okay? I'll tell you whatever you want to know."

"Oh, J.D." Her shoulders sagged. "That's not how it's done."

"Sure it is. I'm offering to talk about my dad. Isn't that what you wanted?"

"You don't get it, do you? It's not what *I* want, it's what *you* want. Sharing personal histories is part of a relationship. It's part of taking off the scabs on your heart for another person. Willingly. Without pressure to do so by anyone. It's not a game of If You Show Me Yours, I'll Show You Mine." She stepped away from him to open the door. "Come on. I'll drive you home."

I am home, he wanted to say. *Here in your kitchen is home.* The room's warmth, the hum of the fridge, the plants on the sink's windowsill, the welcome mat at the back door, the old cupboards, the little wooden table, the yellow walls, the cat curling around her legs…

Home.

Where he couldn't stay.

He followed her back into the winter night.

She was in bed, reading, when her phone rang. A glance told her it was J.D. She had expected his call. On returning to the inn not a word had passed between them. When she pulled to the hotel's curbside, he'd told her that he could manage the pathway alone. And she had let him go, then waited while he walked up the porch steps and into the building. Heart heavy, she drove away.

Before it began, it was done.

How silly of her to have imagined more. *To have let your heart get involved.*

Again.

Relationships were not her thing. *Best get used to your destiny.* Work was her love, her marriage, her baby. What made her think she had time for a man?

But, oh, he was *such* a man. And, if she could admit it, she might have felt a little more than attraction to him. She might have begun, just a little, to fall in love.

The phone was on its final refrain before her voice mail would click in; she grabbed the receiver. "Hello, J.D."

"Sometimes," he said, his voice deep in her ear, "I hate caller ID. I thought you'd let it ring because it was me. Ella, I'm a sorry ass. The way I handled tonight… If you don't want to talk to me again… Hell." She envisioned him pinching the bridge of his nose, running a hand through that lush hair.

"I shouldn't have pushed," she said, trying to find balance with her own emotions. "It wasn't fair." *Considering I barely know you.*

"Can we start over?"

And there it was, the question begging a yes or no that could alter her life's path. If she said yes where would he lead her? If she said no, where would she lead herself?

Already she knew the answer to the second question and it sent a chill across her heart. Saying no would confirm having no life outside of her work and her patients.

There's no one at WRG who remotely interests you.

And in a town the size of Walnut River, with its aging population, how great were her opportunities? J.D. offered a chance at a bit of freedom and fun and excitement.

And more...if she let herself romanticize.

"We can start over," she agreed slowly.

"Great." His relief was audible. "I've decided to follow your recommendation. I'm seeing my father tomorrow."

"Don't do it for me, J.D."

"I know. Do it for myself. And I am. It's time. I had a wake-up call tonight at your house—which, by the way, I'd really like to see beyond the back door."

Though he couldn't see it, she smiled. "You will and you'll be okay tomorrow."

"I hope so."

"Just be yourself. The way you are with me," she added.

At that he chuckled. "If I acted *that* way around him, he'd see me out the door with a shotgun. Ella?"

"Yes?"

"I think we've had our first fight. I've never had a first fight with a woman before."

"Really?"

"I'm ashamed to admit it, but I just didn't care enough to have one. With you it's..." Sigh. "You scare me."

A little jolt hit her stomach. "Ditto."

"Yeah?"

"Don't let it go to your head."

He laughed. "I could take that another way."

"But you won't. Good night, J.D."

"'Night, babe."

For a long while she lay awake, thinking. The days since she had met him in the E.R. were a string of pearls she touched and retouched, turned and rolled in the palm of her memory. She went over conversations, the way he looked at her and she at him.

Until she was back to tonight's phone call—and the fact he wanted to begin again.

J.D. took a cab to his childhood home. *We can start over.* Her voice, soft in his mind. Words he also planned for him and Pops.

The cement driveway had been cleared and sanded. The old man might not be home, but out with his cronies, drinking a beer at the Crab Shack along the river.

Careful with his cane, J.D. took his time to the front door. Sometime in the past five years the house had been painted gold, the shutters dark brown. Near his old bedroom, the red maple reached its stark branches above the roofline; beside the front stoop the hydrangeas outdistanced his own six-three height.

He rang the doorbell, something he'd begun to do when he left and returned that first year.

A long minute later, the door opened. And there was his father's craggy face.

Here the changes were more dramatic. Half a decade could do that to a man's eyes and mouth and hair, his posture. Jared Sumner no longer stood straight and tall. Instead, he leaned on a cane similar to J.D.'s, his bony shoulders sagging in a blue plaid shirt.

But his eyes were still keen as a Fourth of July sky.

"Hey, Pops."

"J.D."

"How you doing?"

"Fine. You're up an' walkin', I see."

"Yeah. Heard you came to the hospital." *Are you going to invite me in, Pops?*

"I did. You were sleepin'."

"Should've woke me."

"Maybe." For several seconds Jared studied J.D.

"Pops? We gonna stand out here in the cold and talk or are you going to let me in?"

The old man jerked. "Oh, yeah. 'Course. Come in." He stepped back, pulling the door wider.

J.D. entered the small foyer, automatically turning left to the coat closet. "Mind if I stay awhile? Or do you have plans?"

"No plans. Hang up your coat." Leaving J.D. to do just that, his dad walked to the kitchen. "Want some coffee, tea? Don't know what you drink anymore."

"Coffee's fine." J.D. shrugged off his coat.

The living room furniture he'd sat on as a kid had been replaced, the TV upgraded to a sixty-inch wall unit. The kitchen, however, astonished him. Quaker cupboards, fresh green paint, new sink, yellow-patterned linoleum.

"Wow, when did you renovate?"

"Couple years ago. Got tired of the dark colors."

"Looks great. Nice and bright."

Jared turned from the counter, eyes full of something

J.D. hadn't seen in a long while, maybe never: pleasure. "Think so?"

"Yeah," he said, meaning it.

"It was Prue's idea."

"Prue? You mean…" J.D. jerked his head left.

"Yup. The same. She's got an eye for things."

J.D. wondered what else she had an eye for. His old man, maybe? "She still live next door?"

"Yup. Husband passed on four years ago."

"Still has the bakeshop, right?"

"Bakeshop and deli now. Belle manages it."

Prudy's daughter, and old classmate of J.D.'s.

He walked to the window opposite a table for two. Across snowy yards was Ella's house. Last night, he'd stood at *her* window viewing his dad's place—and now, here he was. Without thinking, he asked, "Do you know your neighbor across the alley?"

Pops set cloth placemats on the table. Another of Prudy's influences? "Doc Wilder. She's the one who gave me my new hip. Damn fine woman, that one."

J.D. remained at the window. Except for the cat, her house was empty. Ella would be at the hospital, likely in surgery, working those long fingers around someone's distressed bones or joints. The way she had on him. And, evidently, his old man.

No wonder she'd been full of questions. She had recognized similarities. The birthmark on his inner thigh.

"I was wrong, you know." Pops broke into J.D.'s reverie.

Turning, he met the old man's eyes. "In what way?"

"Making you believe hospitals are bad, that they end

your life. I was wrong to put those thoughts in your head
when you were a kid, J.D. I knew it when I took you into
the clinic with that double ear infection when you were
five, an' you cried an' cried that you didn't want to die. I
knew then I'd done wrong."

J.D. shrugged. "I got over it." But he hadn't really.

A week ago he'd sweated through bizarre dreams and
anxiety. Believing he could die any moment. Die quick
like his mother, without warning.

No, he hadn't gotten over it. However, in Ella's care
he'd recognized a difference.

Pops pulled out a chair. "I wanted to tell you when I
came to see you in the hospital."

J.D. noticed his father's hand shake pouring cream into
his mug. He wanted to put a hand on the old man's
shoulder. Instead, he pulled out the opposite chair. "You're
telling me now, Pops. Better late than never, right?"

Jared stirred his coffee. "S'pose. It's a good hospital.
Lotta folks come for miles to get care. There are lineups
for elective surgeries, y'know." He eyed J.D. "Wouldn't
want to see that change."

J.D. held back his surprise. "Why would it change?"

"That's what you're here for, ain't it? To amalgamate
Walnut River General into a bunch of hospitals. You're
wrong, is all I'm sayin'. Walnut River should care for this
town in its own way. Leave it alone, son."

J.D. snorted. As always, his dad was telling him what
to do. Why had he thought today would be different?

Tamping back disillusionment he said, "NHC could
make the hospital more effective with increased surger-

ies per day, for example. Maybe implement a graveyard shift for elective surgeries. *That's* what I'm trying to help with."

His dad shook his head. "Call it what you want. Rumors fly. Prudy hears 'em when she stocks sandwiches in the docters' lounge."

Prudy again. J.D. considered. If he told his father his intentions, good old Prudy could take *those* back to the staff lounge as well.

"Look. Pops. I'm not a bad guy. Walnut River is great, better than great. But there are areas they could improve with updated equipment." *Ours is working just fine,* he could hear Ella scoff. *Why waste money?* Resolutely, he went on, "Furthermore, the hospital could lobby for funding, gain a larger professional base to draw from when they need relief staff. Done with the hospital's current qualities in mind, that could add to it, not detract."

Jared shook his gray head. "Son, you do what you have to do. But this ain't right. You'll be ruinin' a good hospital and makin' a lot of people unhappy, includin' that sweet gal across the way there."

J.D. glanced at Ella's house. *Would* he be ruining her place of work? He reflected on the hospitals NHC had bought out. Efficient institutions today, with little overhead and exceptional equipment. Dammit, Ella *could* use another bone-density scanner. With two, she'd assist more patients, accelerate services.

Suddenly Jared's hand covered J.D.'s. "All I'm asking, J.D., is when you talk to people, listen to what they say. Really listen. Before you put in your report. Will you do that?"

J.D. gazed at his father's work-hardened hand, the knuckles thick and twisted, the veins high and round. A working man's hand.

Shame rose to his throat. "All right. I'll give it a shot."

The doorbell rang. Jared rose and limped from the kitchen. J.D. remained seated. *Jeez.* He thought he'd had the old man pegged all these years. Seemed he didn't know his dad at all.

As a kid, a punk, *could* he have misread Pops?

Murmurs drifted through the house. A woman, a child.

His dad entered. Behind him walked a woman dressed in slacks and a blue sweater that fit her trim body and a little girl, with gold curls to her shoulders, wearing pink overalls. The woman carried a cloth-covered plate.

J.D. stood. He caught Jared's pride at his ingrained manners.

"Remember Mrs. Tavish, son?"

Prudy. "How are you, Mrs. T? It's been a long time."

"It has," she agreed. "But let's forget the formalities, okay? You're no longer a boy and I prefer Prudy." Her smile was honest, happy. "And this…" She brought the child forward. "My granddaughter, Shay. We've been baking all afternoon because today is teachers' in-service and Shay has a day off school. We thought Jared—" Something tender passed between them. "Well, we wanted to share our goodies," she ended, placing the plate on the counter.

"Shay is the best baker." Pops ran a hand over the child's hair and winked. "Aren't you, pint?"

J.D. stared at his dad. Had the old man once winked at him like that? And when had he touched J.D. with such protective care?

A few minutes ago at the table, or did you forget already?

The thought shook J.D.

Pops *had* reached out, there was no denying that handgrip. What else had J.D. forgotten over the years? Had he squelched the good memories because, in his eyes, Pops hadn't acted like the fathers of his school buddies?

Smiling, Jared led the girl to the table. Prudy dug orange juice from the fridge as if it was the most natural thing to do in another person's house.

"Sit, Prue." Pops pointed to the chair J.D. had vacated. "Wanna grab another mug an' the coffeepot, son?"

J.D. did as asked. He couldn't recall Jared ever having a woman to his table. Occasionally, he'd let J.D. have school pals over, and sometimes his cronies from work, but never a woman. To J.D. his old man had been a hard-ass without a soft bone in his body.

After retrieving the coffeepot, he excused himself and went down the hallway to his old bedroom. The door stood open.

Here, nothing had changed. His football jersey still hung on the wall above the bed, his baseball cap sat on the dresser. Track-and-field medals and mystery novels lined the shelves. The bed was the narrow twin mattress he had slept in since he turned two. Why hadn't the old man changed his room when he'd renovated the rest of the house?

"You came home so seldom."

J.D. startled. Pops had followed him into the room. "I

wanted to keep a little part of you with me. Stupid, I know. I shoulda packed up your stuff, put it in the attic."

"I'm glad you didn't," J.D. said hoarsely.

"Yeah?"

"Yeah." And suddenly a waterfall of history he'd forgotten streamed through his mind....

Playing baseball, his dad standing on the sidelines, encouragement in his eyes. Scoring a touchdown and Jared in the bleachers, yelling his name. His old man's hands, his gardener's hands, reaching around J.D.'s ten-year-old shoulders, helping cast a line into the river on a summer's afternoon.

Pain lodged in his chest.

The old man loved him.

It was on his face and in the memories tethered to this room.

He had to get out of here, to reassess God-knew-what. "Look," he said. "I gotta head back to the Inn."

"So soon? You just got here."

"Need to finish some work." His business case waited.

"If you wanna stay in your old room…"

J.D. shook his head. "Can't, Pops."

Stepping around his dad, he walked out of the room.

A minute later, he was outside, buttoning up against a sudden cold wind that bit his face.

Chapter Ten

J.D. sat on the edge of his bed at the inn, cell phone in hand. He'd been mulling over what happened on Birch Avenue for an hour. *If you wanna stay in your old room…* The emotion behind the old man's words tumbled hard through J.D.'s chest.

They had connected in that room. On some level they had connected. Pops wasn't the badass J.D. had always assumed he was. He was a man who had tried to make a home for his kid the only way he knew how.

A man who loved that kid deeper than J.D. had believed.

Before he changed his mind and hooked his cell phone to his belt, he punched in the familiar number.

His father picked up immediately—as if he'd been sitting right by the phone, waiting. "'Lo."

J.D. swallowed. "Hey, Pops."

"Son. Glad you called."

"You alone?"

"Yeah. Prue and Shay left right after you."

Probably because Prudy thought she'd interrupted a father-son bonding moment. J.D. closed his eyes. "Sorry," he said. "Didn't mean for them to run out on you." *Like I did.*

"They didn't. Prue understands things."

No doubt better than J.D. "Look," he said and his throat constricted. "I'm glad we got together, you know? It was nice."

The line was quiet for several beats before Pops said, "You're taller than I was at your age, bigger in the shoulders."

J.D. released a small laugh. "Must be all those New York steaks."

"Got your mother's hair…the way it whipped in the wind. Sun catches it the same, too. Guess you hadn't expected me to keep your room the same, huh?"

"No, Pops. It surprised me." After all the reno work throughout the house.

"Shoulda been a better father when I had the chance," Jared remarked. "Been kinder, gentler. Like I am with Shay."

"Dad—"

"Let me finish. I made us strangers with nothin' in common 'cept our names. I ain't making excuses 'cause I was the adult, the role model." He grunted. "Some role model."

J.D. pressed his fingers to his eyes. "Don't punish yourself."

"Didn't teach you what I shoulda. You're thirty-six years old, a good-lookin' kid, yet you ain't married. So I'm bettin' you're scared to get in deep with a woman. Scared of what might happen to her."

J.D. swallowed. Pops was paring back layers he hadn't recognized. Could it be possible?

Gruffly, Jared continued, "If I'da showed you more affection the way a dad should…"

"You did, Pops. You showed me in a lot of ways. You may not have said the words, but you showed me. Go look at that stuff in my room, and think about the memories."

"I do. Every day."

J.D. was silent. What could he say to take away the guilt in his father's voice? "Pops, listen. There comes a time a kid has to take responsibility, teach himself the ways of life."

"When Gracie died," his dad continued, on a mission now. "When she died, part of my heart died with her. I'd look into your face, see those same green eyes, and it scared the hell out of me. I had no idea how to raise you alone. My old man—" Jared cleared his throat. "He taught me never to show my feelings when things got tough. A man persevered. He shut his mouth, got the job done. I did that with you and it wasn't right. Wasn't right at all."

J.D briefly closed his eyes. Three-and-a-half decades and he'd never heard his father speak with so much emotion. "Pops, you don't need to do this." *You don't need to tear out your guts for me.*

A ragged sigh drifted through the phone. "Yeah, son, I do. I owe you an explanation that's been way too long in coming."

J.D.'s heart banged his ribs. "Maybe we could start fresh."

"I'd like that," Pops said slowly. "I'd like that a lot."

The grin stretching across J.D.'s face hurt. "It's a deal."

After their last botched dinner two days ago, Ella wondered if he'd decided to go back to New York, after all. Twice she'd been tempted to call Ashley, see if he still attended physio, but she didn't want to appear interested—either to J.D. or the hospital staff.

She stayed up until eleven every night telling herself she wasn't waiting for his call, but catching up on her reading. Then one night, lying under the quilt, propped by pillows, *The New England Journal of Medicine* in her lap, she realized she'd read the same paragraph about chronic osteomyelitis a dozen times.

Late in the afternoon on the third day, she sat in her car at the intersection of Lexington and River Road, waiting for the light to change—and debating. Should she turn left, pass the inn? Or continue straight to her side of town?

The light flashed green. Though traffic was slower because of the snowfall that began an hour earlier, Ella pushed the accelerator, intent on home, but halfway through the intersection, she swung left.

Hands tight on the steering wheel, she drove down the road with its big trees, until the inn's lamppost came into view. No gray rental stood in the guest parking. Had he checked out? Or was he still at the hospital, gathering names, slumbering in the solarium? She hadn't ventured near that room since…

Eyes on the road, she drove past the inn.

Pathetic, Ella. He's probably in New York and here you are, driving by like a teenager wanting a glimpse of the school hottie.

She so needed a life.

And groceries.

Pulling into the New England Ranch Market at the next light, she caught sight of Simone Garner, their top E.R. nurse, heading for her vehicle, a sack in each hand.

"Simone," Ella called, stepping from her car.

The nurse had worked at WRG for fifteen years and her kindness and skill was renowned throughout the community. Ella regarded her as a good friend.

Suddenly, she missed her sister Anna fiercely. She missed their camaraderie and girl talks. She missed being able to say *Tell me what to do about J.D.* Seeing Simone sent a sharp spear of yearning through Ella for that kinship with another woman.

Abruptly, she hugged the nurse. "How are you?" she asked, stepping back quickly, embarrassed by her display. "I haven't seen you in a while." Her rotation and Simone's often went in opposite directions for weeks.

Simone's brown eyes smiled. "I've had extra shifts, which my dog has not enjoyed in the least. But—" She chuckled. "Today I'm off, so he's happy. You?"

Ella brushed at her bangs. "Crazy busy. Can't seem to get ahead of the lineup some days."

"Don't tell Sumner, that rep prowling the hospital. He'll take it to NHC's bank and we'll find ourselves sold to the highest bidder."

"J.D.'s not like that."

Simone blinked. "Ella, he may be your patient, but he's also a snitch for that corporation."

"Snitch? That's an awfully strong word."

But a niggle of doubt hovered. Was Simone right? Could there be more to that discussion at the Dakota last week? Intentions that, perhaps, weren't as on par as Ella had thought? Argh. She was so confused about the man. "I have to go," she said, starting for the electronic doors of the store.

Simone caught her arm. "Ella, I'm sorry, but—"

"Look, I'm just tired and want to get home." *Where I can think and put some sense to all this.*

"If you need to talk, I'm here."

"I know. Thanks, Simone, but I'm okay. See you later." She hurried across the parking lot, through falling flakes that, in the lamplight, materialized big as the cotton ball in her throat.

By the time she walked into the back door of her cozy little house on Cedar Avenue, her kitchen clock read 6:45 p.m., and Molly leaned against her legs. "Hey, my little fan. I love you, too." She hauled the cat into her arms.

Ten minutes later, the groceries put away, Molly fed and the cat box cleaned, Ella stood in the bathroom, washing her hands. The mirror revealed dark circles under her eyes. When her stomach growled, she realized breakfast had been her last meal.

"If you're not careful, you'll be the one in a hospital bed," she muttered to her reflection.

Would J.D. care?

J.D.'s gone.

Deflated, she dried her hands and returned to the kitchen to heat a plate of leftover lasagna and toss a small salad.

The dishes cleared and cleaned after her meal, she loaded the washing machine and ironed a blouse for tomorrow. By the time she crawled under the covers it was almost ten.

About to turn out the light, the family photo on her dresser caught her eye. Taken twelve years ago in her parents' backyard, she remembered the moment as if she had just stepped into the cluster of her family and her mom had just put an arm around her waist. Ella, Alice, James and Anna stood in the first row, with David and Peter behind.

David had one hand on Ella's shoulder and one on their mother's. Beside Alice stood James, patriarch of both family and Walnut River General. Ella could see the tips of his fingers around Anna's waist; Peter's hands clasped her shoulder and their father's.

A day of celebration for Peter's completed internship, the photographer had taken a dozen group photos, each with family members trading places. Ella loved this photo because her mother had hugged her close and given her a little squeeze and David had teased in her ear, *Smile so we know how much you love pictures,* just before the camera had clicked its shot. Ella's lips tugged. At seventeen she'd hated having her photo taken. Back then, her glasses, braces and near-flat chest cried out *nerd.*

Anna, on the other hand, looked like a Scandinavian goddess with her lovely white-blond hair and sky-blue eyes. At eighteen she had the figure of a siren. Full breasts, tiny waist, long, shapely legs.

Anna, whom James and Alice adopted before Ella was born, had been the closest to Ella—even through their sibling rivalry and those catcalls of loser and bitch.

Such teenage drama, she thought, her gaze falling on Anna's Mona Lisa smile. Not for the first time, Ella wondered what had been going through her sister's mind in that photo.

Smiling at the camera, had Anna known then medicine wasn't her gig? *Oh, Anna. There's so much I want to share with you.*

Except those days were done. She and Anna hadn't talked, really talked, in almost ten years. Not since her sister's first year of med school when she marched into Ella's bedroom and shouted, *I'm not doctor material. I don't have that kind of rhino skin. Why can't anyone get that?* Then she'd stormed out of the house and driven to a friend's place. A week later she moved to New York.

Aw, Anna. You always got woozy at the sight of your own scrapes and cuts, and cried when you saw an animal in pain. Poor dad. He thought you'd outgrow it.

Worse were the family gatherings. James, Peter, David—*and me,* she admitted—talking shop: hospitals, patients, medicine. Standing apart, Anna would wait for someone to notice her, to say, *Hey, what's going on with you in the Big Apple, sis?*

Was it any wonder her sister rarely came home anymore?

Ella glanced at her phone. *Call her*, a tiny voice whispered. *Take the first step, start making things right.* The way she had with J.D. and his dad.

"What do you think, Molly?" Squinty yellow eyes blinked and a mouth full of tiny, sharp teeth yawned widely. "Right. It's up to me."

Quickly she dialed her sister's number. "Anna?" Ella began when her sister answered.

"Hi."

One word, hanging in mid-space. "How—how are you?"

"Fine. You?"

"Busy." *Come on, Ella. You wanted to talk, so talk!* "Real busy with the weather and snow and…" *Oh, God.*

"What's up, Ella? I know it's not the weather."

Yes, it is! Why can't we talk about the weather? We should be able to talk about anything! "I want things back to the way they were between us," she blurted.

A sigh whispered through the line. "You can't bring back the past, El. You know that. It's best to leave things alone."

"Don't you miss us?" Now that they were speaking, Ella was determined to get to the bottom of this *thing* separating them. "I miss you, dammit. C'mon, Anna, talk to me. Why are you avoiding us?"

"Us? As in you and the boys over there, and me over here?"

Ella swallowed a swell of ire. "I can't believe you just said that. Don't you get that we love you? We *all* miss you. You and I used to be so close, we shared everything.

I miss that. I want to know what's going on in your life. I want to share what's going on in mine, that I'm—" Before she spewed regretful words, Ella shut up.

"What's going on with you?" Her sister's voice softened.

"Nothing. It doesn't matter." *I think I'm falling for a guy who's on the wrong side of the fence. And I want to sleep with him, but he's had women—and I've never done it.*

Humiliation washed through her. How could she explain *that* to her sister? Here she was almost thirty *and a doctor*, and a man hadn't touched her in that way, not once. The idea of spilling her guts about J.D. brought on an unexpected shyness.

"I can't talk about it," she said, heart heavy.

"Does it concern a man?"

Oh, yes. Anna knew her well. "I—I don't want to talk about it," she repeated.

"All right. Sure." Her sister's voice cooled.

"Don't get in a huff. It's hard for me to explain because…." *I feel abandoned by you.* "I don't know if you'll be here all the time."

"Emotionally, you mean?"

"Yes."

Pause. "Maybe we should try and rebuild."

"Can we?" Ella asked.

"Maybe with small steps."

She closed her eyes, took a sustaining breath. "Anna, I've never…" *Slept with a man.*

"Never what? Felt this way about a guy?"

"No."

"Is he a local? Someone I would know?"

"He grew up here, but he lives and works in New York now. For some health-care company."

A weighty quiet descended through the line. "Anna?"

"What company?"

"Northeastern HealthCare. He— The man in question is collecting all kinds of data about Walnut River General."

"I see."

"Peter thinks they're trying to take over the hospital. Sometimes I believe him and sometimes I don't know what to think. Personally, I just want to do my job and forget all this gibberish."

"Then that's what you do."

"What if Peter's right, though? What if this man's trying to manipulate us for his corporation?"

"I can't answer that, Ella. I'm not there. Look, it's late and I have an early meeting in the morning."

"Sure," she said, taken back by Anna's abruptness.

"Let's keep in touch."

"OK. 'Night, Anna."

"Goodbye."

The line disconnected. Ella stared at the photograph. Goodbye.

As if she were a stranger.

If Anna had said *don't count on me* she couldn't be more clear. Ella sighed. Why had she expected more? Because tonight she'd tried to reach out, tried to mend the hole in the bridge of time. Except Anna hadn't followed. The moment Ella mentioned Peter and the hospital her sister withdrew.

Heart sore, Ella shut off the lamp. She was no closer to connecting with Anna than she was at figuring out J.D.

Peter met her in the hallway as she headed for the O.R. the next morning to repair a forty-year-old man's fractured tibia.

"'Morning, El," her brother said, falling in step. "Can you meet Simone, Bethany and me in the cafeteria at eleven? I'm buying. Though you might not like what's on the menu."

Peter's dark eyes were serious. He wasn't talking food lists.

"What's up?" But she knew before he said the name.

"J. D. Sumner. See you when you're done." On a quick heel, her brother turned and strode back the way they had come, white lab coat fanning behind his long legs.

Ninety minutes later, with the patient in recovery, Ella headed for the change room to tug on a black skirt, pink blouse and lab coat for her afternoon appointments— and the cafeteria meeting.

Heads bent together, Peter and Bethany sat at a corner table.

Thank God for small favors, Ella thought. *About time my big brother found a mate.*

He was forty, his youth flying into the wind. *Like mine.*

The thought pricked. They were here to talk about J.D. and she'd guarantee it wasn't because he haunted her dreams.

She pulled out the chair across from Peter. "Hey, lovebirds."

Bethany smiled into his eyes. "Are we lovebirds?"

"You bet," he affirmed. Had they been alone, Ella believed her brother would have kissed the beautiful redhead. Instead, he straightened and glanced at Ella. "How was the surgery?"

"Good. Patient has a strong left leg again."

Dressed in nurses' scrubs, Simone Garner squeezed in beside Ella. "Did everyone eat already?"

Ten minutes later, salads, sandwiches and bowls of minestrone soup decked the table. Peter said, "You three are the only people I can discuss this with."

This. Ella had no doubt he meant NHC. His gaze on Ella, Peter continued. "For the record, J. D. Sumner is no longer your patient. I checked. Apparently, he's had his files transferred to Springfield and is seeing a doctor there. Do you know why?"

"He…um… Look, it's personal." And it was. Her private life did not belong to her family.

"What is said here, stays here," Peter stated.

Ella darted a look at the other two women. "All right," she began cautiously. "He asked me out, but because he is—*was*—my patient, I wouldn't go."

Peter's eyes were steady. "And did you? Once he transferred?"

Ella sat back in her chair. "Okay, is this an inquisition on my character, Peter? Because if it is, I'm out of here."

He shook his head. "I'm just trying to see where you stand before we go further."

"Where *I* stand? I hope you're not insinuating something nasty because if you are, Peter, you and I need to have a private chat."

"Hear, hear," Bethany said. Her expression held empathy for Ella and reproof for Peter.

He stared at his plate. "Okay, I screwed up. Sorry."

Bethany set a hand on his arm. "Whether or not she's dating J.D. isn't our concern, Peter." She glanced across the table. "I'm sure Ella will be on our side about this."

This, again. Her hands cold in her lap, Ella said, "The last thing I want is for our hospital to be put on a chopping block."

Peter nodded grimly. "We know NHC has done similar machinations with other small medical centers through-out New England. NHC comes in subtly and before you know it, the hospital becomes part of the corporation."

Simone shifted in her chair. "A patient who moved here last year said it happened to the hospital in her hometown. Tenure staff were replaced with new doctors and nurses."

"That," Peter said adamantly, "isn't going to happen at Walnut River General."

"What about the fraud claims?" Bethany asked.

"Exactly," Peter intoned. "We need to find out if these claims are coming out of the woodwork to make WRG look inefficient."

Ella set down her salad fork. Both Peter and West MacGregor had implied that J.D. was involved in the fraud claims. Still, she could not picture him as a delib-erately malicious man.

"What are you saying, Peter?" she asked, holding his gaze. "That Mr. Sumner is the root of the problem?"

Her brother stabbed a shred of lettuce. "I don't know. But I do know we could lose our hospital if we sit on our hands."

"What do you propose?"

For a long minute no one said a word. Their plates and bowls sat half empty, untouched.

Simone offered, "We could go to the media."

"The media?" Bethany blinked. "They'd have a free-for-all with this kind of information."

"Not if we play it right." Peter leaned forward. "Ella, you help Rev. Blackwell with the homeless on Sundays. What if we get the *Courier* to write a story about that? Who knows, maybe we can get patients and families to rally behind the hospital in other ways. It would give us a fighting chance, at least."

She winced. "I don't like the idea of using people, Peter. And neither would Oliver Blackwell."

"Will you feel the same when your level of care is diluted due to a bunch of rotating surgeons selected by NHC?"

Please, no, she thought. But wasn't it what J.D. had alluded to, if NHC took over? More medical staff, more equipment? Was that why he'd asked if she would one day work in a larger hospital where all types of opportunities were available?

Gut instinct said J.D. wouldn't deceive her. They had shared bits of their histories, they had laughed. *Kissed.* He wouldn't use her.

Stubbornly, she pushed back the possibility, and her chair. "I have to get to work."

"Think about our proposition, Ella," Peter said. "We have to fight this somehow."

"I know." Stomach in a clench, she hurried from the cafeteria.

Chapter Eleven

Growing up, J.D. had sauntered down Lexington Avenue a thousand times, knew every store, every shop. Over the years some had disappeared, changed owners, changed stock; others had facelifts; still others retained the identifying marks of bygone years.

One was Prudy's Menu.

Around five on Thursday afternoon, he parked the rental at the New England Ranch Market and walked to the shop he had visited as a kid, where Prudy once baked her famous cookies and squares.

Swept clean of snow, the sidewalks were alive with people hurrying home to family and loved ones. The notion stuck like a wad of tissue in his gut. When had he last hurried home to someone at the end of the day? Not since he'd been a kid in grade school, hoping for a simple *How was your day, boy?* from his old man.

So why walk the street to the shop where Prudy worked?

Why this urge to connect with his past?

Hadn't he done that when he knocked on Pops' door? Saw Prudy and her grandkid? Saw his old bedroom?

J.D.'s chest constricted. In a skewed way, his old man loved him. Had always loved him—if those memories resurrected in his old bedroom meant anything—like the time Jared took him to the bake shop and bought a chocolate chip cookie four inches in diameter.

Jerking to a stop, J.D. stared at the yellow script announcing Prudy's Menu above the old wooden door. How had he forgotten?

He'd been eight, helping Jared in the gardens of an upscale residence on the north side of town. On the way home, with dirt on their clothes, the old man had stopped at Prudy's, bought him the cookie. *Y' done good today, boy.* And Pops handed him the treat.

Sparse and rare, the old man's compliments were long-lost treasures buried but preserved forever.

Trouble was, as a mutinous teenager he'd piled a load of loneliness on top of those treasures, sinking them so deep he'd forgotten each word—and the emotions attached to them.

Hell. If ever there was a head case, here he stood.

Ella should find him fascinating as a partner. *Partner?* Where the hell had that come from?

But he knew. From the moment he'd tumbled down those hospital steps, the journey into his past had been a strong arm directing him to things as they *were*, rather than the dark illusions he'd conjured for eighteen years.

Yes, he was successful, ambitious and, at times, insensitive. But he was also...*lonely.* He shook his head to dislodge the emotion burning deep inside. Partner. The word hung in the winter air, mellow as a puff of warm smoke, entreating, enticing, evolving.

Partner...friend...mate...lover...

On a soft curse, he pushed through Prudy's door. The bell above tinkled pleasantly, a reminder two decades old.

Standing on the threshold, J.D. took in the alterations: green bistro tables along the front windows; a raised platform with its railing covered in live vines; a mural of the Berkshire Mountains.

At the soda counter on the right stood Prudy's daughter, the girl he'd gone to school with.

"Hey, Belle," he said, walking over. "Long time no see."

She gave him a sharp look. "J.D.? Hey! Heard you were in town. Your dad's over the moon you're home."

"Yeah." Suddenly uncomfortable, he checked the menu with its fancy script on the wall chalkboard behind the counter. "Wouldn't mind a turkey club."

"Sure. Fries or salad?"

"Both. And I'll take a cinnamon roll as well." He dug out his wallet, laid the bills on the counter. "Keep the change."

"Well, thanks, J.D.," Belle said, punching the order into a computerized till, another update. Over her shoulder she called to the open kitchen door, "Fergus, order in." To J.D. she said, "My beloved." And she smiled. Not husband, *beloved*. "Fergus," she yelled again. "Come out here for a sec. Want you to meet someone."

A man in a long white apron stepped from the kitchen. "You bellowed, darlin'?" he inquired, a twitch to his lips.

"This here's J.D. Used to live next door to us. Jared's son."

Fergus offered a hand, a grin. "So. You're the elusive son. Wouldn't've known Jared had a kid but for Belle and Prudy."

"Yeah." J.D. shrugged. "I don't get back much."

"Well, hopefully that'll change. Hey, if you ever want to do some fishing, let me know. Got a cabin along the Hoosic, if you like rainbow trout."

"Thanks." J.D. swallowed hard. Small-town generosity. All the years he had lived in New York, not a single friend or colleague doled out friendship as Fergus did, a man who took him in simply because he knew Belle and Prudy and Pops. "I'll keep it in mind."

"Looking forward to it. Club to go or stay?"

"To go."

"Coming right up."

"J.D.?"

Her soft, feminine voice had him snapping around.

"Ella. Where…?" And then, beyond her shoulder he noticed the leather sofa, cushy chairs, the gas fireplace on the raised platform. And the blond man sitting on the couch, watching them.

"I'm doing an interview for the *Walnut River Courier*."

"Oh?" he said, noticing the way her dark hair swung

loose above the collar of her green sweater. A sweater molding breasts that enticed a man's hands to… He glared in the direction of the couch. "On what?"

"The hospital and its community." Not catching the nip of jealousy in his voice, she smiled. "How a number of our staff works with the less fortunate."

Once more she surprised him. He glanced at the young reporter whose notes were spread across the coffee table. "Does that include you?" J.D. asked refocusing on her.

"I work with the church's soup kitchen every Sunday if I'm not on call. Several of my patients are Reverend Blackwell's customers. I like to make sure they're healing properly."

"As in a pro bono assurance?"

"Yes."

He was more than intrigued. "Where else do you volunteer?"

"Wherever I can. I may be an orthopedic surgeon, J.D., but I'm a doctor first. Patients can't always make it in to my office."

"You make house calls?"

"Sometimes."

His mouth tugged into a smile. "The way you give patients a ride home?" The way she'd offered to shuttle him back to the inn when he could have taken a taxi.

"It's part of who I am, part of what our hospital is about. Peter does the same, as do other doctors and nurses. WRG is a community-based hospital, which means we service the people of our town not just with our professional skills, but also with empathy." She raised a shapely brow. "But for a man hoping to change those standards into drive-through services, it's probably difficult to understand."

He couldn't help the twinge of guilt—then anger. "Who told you that? As I've mentioned before, NHC would like nothing more than to upgrade Walnut River General. Which includes your unit, Ella. Either way, you'll benefit."

She smiled sadly. "Multimillion-dollar companies like NHC don't upgrade out of the goodness of their hearts. There's always an ulterior motive, and those motives are buyouts."

"Would that be so awful?" he asked quietly when he noticed the reporter leaning forward, trying to catch their conversation. "The hospital would have only good things to gain." At least that's what he hoped. For her sake.

"And everything to lose. Look, I need to finish this interview."

He caught her arm before she walked away. "Can we talk later?"

"I'm going home after this. I haven't eaten, nor has Molly."

"I'll bring some Chinese." When she would've protested he set a finger against her soft mouth. "We never did get the chance to eat with chopsticks."

Belle set a brown paper sack on the counter. "I'll see you at your house in an hour," he told Ella as he grabbed his meal.

"You plan to eat a sandwich *and* takeout? You must be famished." She laughed.

Oh, he was famished, all right. For her. So much so he ached with the prospect of nibbling on her delicious lips...and other parts. "I'll see you soon." A nod to Belle, he left the shop.

And smiled all the way back to the inn.

True to his word, J.D. rang her front doorbell an hour later. After he'd left the deli, she had wanted nothing more than to end the interview with Phil and rush home. The reporter had given her odd looks the moment J.D. walked from the shop. The one question she had granted him was, "Is that the NHC rep?" to which she had replied, "Yes, and that's as far as we'll go with that topic." She wasn't sure whom she wanted to protect: J.D. or WRG.

She hoped Peter would like the interview. She'd explained the hospital's volunteer program embracing the methods of care and skill the doctors used to make the process of healing as gentle and easy as possible for their patients.

She'd talked about giving back massages to long-term bedridden patients and rubbing lotions into chapped skin and sores. She talked about medical staff—including her—waiting at a bedside to ensure patients took their meds. She mentioned how, if no one was available, doctors changed sweat-soaked gowns and linens and fluffed pillows—all for the comfort of the patient.

She had talked until she was drained.

And then J.D., in that dangerously elegant long black coat, walked into the shop and her heart had flown against her ribs.

And it still beat like a toy drum as she hurried to the front door.

Upon arriving home, she had debated whether to slip into something sexier…a dress, perhaps.

In the end, she'd forfeited sex appeal for what he saw at Prudy's Menu: green knit top, chocolate cords. Although she did reapply her makeup and run a brush through her hair.

He stood on the stoop holding a cardboard box from Ling Hu's in one hand and a potted hot-pink orchid in the other. A bottle of wine poked from under his arm.

A few snowflakes clung to the black wool across his big shoulders and winked in the red-brown depths of his hair. It had begun to snow again.

"We eating in the doorway, Doc?" he asked, levity gleaming between his black lashes.

"Sorry. Come in." As she stepped aside, J.D. entered her cramped foyer. The door was barely closed when he set his gifts on the tiny table opposite the coat closet, turned and took her face between his hands.

"I've been waiting for days." And then he kissed her.

At first a touch of lips, then he sank in to stay.

The kiss was mobile and wet and so erotic, Ella caught his wrists simply to hang on. With a burst of clarity she thought, *This is how it'll be in bed with him.*

Somewhere in the back of her mind, she became aware of his hands, running over her shoulders, down the slope of her spine to her hips. He walked her backward three steps, until she was flat against the door and his hands were on her face again, in her hair and he maneuvered her mouth in a race of need.

"Ella," he groaned, his hands everywhere, tripping everywhere. "You drive me crazy. *Crazy*."

"Same," she whispered. Quivering, her nerves sensitized to the point of pain, she pushed at the lapels of his coat. She had to feel him, had to free him of that barrier keeping her fingers and palms from the warmth of his flesh.

Lips joined, he offered aid, shrugging from the wool, tossing it onto the pony-wall dividing the entrance and her living room. Then, he boosted her to that pony-wall and he set his lips to the flesh over her collarbones and sucked gently.

"You shouldn't have lifted me," she said. "Your knee—"

"To hell with my knee," he muttered between kisses. "Where's your bedroom?"

Just like that, she froze—and understood he sensed something had gone off-center.

"Ella, what is it?"

She was still wrapped around his waist, around his neck, where she hid her face. Oh, she wanted him. Her body cried with it. Twenty steps and they would be in her bedroom. Twenty seconds and he'd be inside her.

A first for her. But not, she knew, for him.

What would he think of her, an almost-thirty doctor and still as naive as she was at thirteen?

Weird, that's what he'd think. Ella, the doctor who's stood witness to countless naked bodies, but never had a man in her bed.

The more she thought of it, the more certain she became that he would wonder and question her failure at the male-female connection, question her inability to attract a man before this moment.

Worse, what if he saw her behavior as a ruse to keep him from reporting whatever information he was gathering to NHC? After all, he had seen her with a newsman this afternoon.

J.D. eased her face from the crook of his neck. "Honey, what's wrong?" Worry darted over his features.

She lowered her gaze to the collar of his rust-colored shirt. "We need to slow down, J.D." Slipping from his waist, she said, "I'm not ready for this. I'm sorry."

They remained at the pony-wall, his groin against her stomach where she felt the rise in him, the solidity, and she heaved a sigh. She had failed with a man once more.

Maybe she should hire an escort and just…get the deed done. That way men like J.D. wouldn't think her an intimacy oddball.

A frigid oddball.

Gently, he lifted her chin, his eyes warm and a little amused. "Why don't we eat that takeout before it gets cold? Nothing worse than chilly chow mein." He kissed her nose, helped her to the floor, and stepped away to collect his coat from where it had slid to the hardwood.

They set up in her kitchen. Molly, on the scent of sweet-and-sour chicken, twined around Ella's legs with disgruntled meows.

"You've already had your dinner," Ella told the little cat. "Be content. It's not nice to be greedy."

Chuckling, J.D. popped the wine. "At least she asks. Colleague of mine has a cat that snitches scraps from the table. He can't seem to train it to stop. So…I don't eat at his house anymore." He shot Ella a look. "Don't get me wrong. I like animals. A lot. But I'm not into sharing my placemat with them."

"Table manners are a learned art for all species." She set his beautiful orchid on the table. "I meant to thank you for this, by the way. I wasn't being neglectful."

He shrugged. "We were a little busy at the time."

Ella ducked her head. "I've never been that distracted before."

Holding two glasses of chardonnay, he came up behind her, laid his mouth against her neck. "The thought turns me on. You, distracted because of me."

"Exhibiting your ego again, Mr. Sumner?" But a thrill toured her spine.

He set the glasses on the table, caught her lips with his. "No ego, sweetheart. Just in lust with you, is all."

In lust. Two words, and he'd leveled her again. "J.D."

"The way you say my name…" He cupped her cheek. "Makes me want to take you right here, right now. All night."

She thought he would kiss her again, but no, he gave her a half smile instead and touched his thumb to her chin, then removed the waxy boxes from the sack, opened their lids, eliciting the pungent scent of takeout.

Although her insides quivered, Ella drew a pair of blue plates from a cupboard. "Our own blue-plate special," she said, her heart bumping hard at the sight of him at her table.

Truth was, no man had sat at this table, not even Peter.

J.D. was the first. And if she was to admit another truth, J.D. was the first in many aspects of her life. The first to woo her with a simple look. The first she dreamed about at night. The first she pictured touching her when she stood in the shower.

The first she imagined making her a woman.

Was love at first sight possible?

She looked over at him, saw how the soft lighting graced his cheeks and jaw and broad shoulders, pitched flames into the richness of his hair—and she fell.

She fell long and hard and down and down, into the vortex of his forest eyes and…

Oh, my God. I'm in love with him.

It wasn't a matter of pondering—Yes? No?—but a matter of reality, of conviction. She sat back stunned.

J.D. paused, chopsticks perched over his plate. "Ella?" A deep crease slashed between his brows.

She blinked. "I'm…You're…Thank you for the food and wine," she stammered, unable to think lucidly. "They're delicious."

"You're welcome. So what's really on your mind?"

"I realized I've been very remiss tonight."

"Are you thinking about how my presence at your kitchen table will affect our relationship at the hospital?"

Cold as rain water. And she was glad for the dousing. She dove right in. "The hospital has nothing to do with my personal life."

He looked around, came back to her. "From what I've seen, your personal life is the hospital. When have you taken a break, Doc? An honest-to-God vacation that lasted more than a weekend? Hell, come to think of it, when have you gone away for a weekend? Seems to me that hospital is eating up your life. Even on your days off you volunteer at soup kitchens and the abused women's shelter."

When her brows jumped, he offered a rueful smile. "I have my sources." He reached across the table, caught her hands. "You're a great doctor, Ella. Brilliant, in fact, and for that my knee will always be grateful, but I'm going to offer you some time away. Come to Vermont with me."

"Vermont?"

"I have a cottage across the state line, about fifteen miles off Highway 7 in Bennington County. Place is a little rustic, but it's quiet, with no phone except my cell, which I turn off. And the only visitors are squirrels, deer, birds and a bear or two. What do you say?"

She pulled her hands from his, picked up her chop-sticks. "I don't know…"

"Tomorrow is Valentine's Day. Are you doing anything special?"

"I'm working a shift for another doctor who needs some time…" *Away with his wife.*

Time away. Exactly what J.D. inferred.

She toyed with a spring roll on her plate. He was right. She didn't take time off. Because she loved her job.

Wrong, Ella. It's because you have no significant other. That's why you make the hospital your home. And maybe that was what Tyler had known four years ago. *Except I never loved Tyler.*

J.D. sat back in his chair, shook his head. "Working

an extra shift. Doc, what good will you be to your patients if you're worn out with exhaustion?"

"I'm not exhausted. I sleep well every night."

"Eight hours?"

"Enough to do my job perfectly."

"I didn't say you couldn't. I'm a walking example. But maybe WRG needs a larger medical base to offset doctors needing a break."

She held his gaze. "One NHC would propose?"

"It's not an evil company, Doc. There is a plus side. However, Henry Weisfield, your hospital administrator, is not one. He's a few months from retirement, which means he's been on golf-course mode for the past two or three years."

Ella leaned forward. "So he's expendable in your view?"

"Considering he doesn't have a ten-year capital-expenditure plan, yes. And does he care? No, because he's leaving. With all due respect, those are not good prospects. Therefore, I hope your board comes up with a damn good administrator to replace him. At least one who'll make sure doctors like you get some downtime by increasing support staff to augment the rising number of patients. As you know, this town has a large population of seniors—my dad included. WRG won't be able to handle the eventual overload if it's not prepared."

Ella rested her arms along the edge of the table. "I'd heard Henry was on your side."

J.D. shrugged. "One day he is, the next not. He agrees with whomever he's spoken with last."

"Doesn't want to rock the boat during his last couple

of months on the job," she murmured. What they needed was someone who could take on NHC, someone with medical and hospital knowledge and expertise in the boardroom. Most of all, they needed the applicant to understand the workings of *their* hospital.

Thankful she had done the story with the *Walnut River Courier*, Ella wondered how J.D. might view the article that touted the hospital's legacy left by her father. Possibly, the man sitting across from her would not agree with James Wilder's "old-fashioned" methods of medical practices, those she had described and explained to the eager reporter. There was also the chance J.D. would regard the story as a means of playing public sympathy to thwart NHC's plans.

Either way, she wouldn't win the argument.

"Maybe," she quipped, "you should apply for the job."

He studied her for a long moment. "Maybe I should."

Her heart kicked. Mercy, had she lost it, suggesting such a thing? If J.D. applied and courted the board into thinking he was the man they needed, he would turn the entire operation over to NHC without a second's thought. He had no vested interest in maintaining the standards set by her father. Yes, his allegiance was to NHC, but… Her breath caught. What if her article placed a splinter of doubt in his mind about NHC's initiative? Dare she hope her words might make a difference?

The more she thought about the situation, the more disillusioned she became. She was in love with a man who could and likely would pigeonhole her hospital into something she would end up hating. She knew it as sure as she was sitting at her table this minute, bumping toes with J.D.

They finished the meal in silence. Done, he helped clear away the dishes. "I'll do them later," she said, heading for the front entrance and his coat.

He chuckled. "In a hurry to get rid of me, Doc?"

"No, just tired." Which was true. She needed a month of sleep.

His eyes turned serious. "Think about that trip to Vermont. It's only forty-five minutes away."

It did sound delicious. And to be with J.D. an entire weekend...

Emotion lodged in her throat and her blood ran thick. After such a weekend, she would not come home a maid.

In a bold move, she wrapped her arms around his neck, and tucked her face into the vee of his shirt where the scent of his skin made her fall harder. Confusion riddled her mind as tears burned behind her eyes. She knew it was wrong to want him, but impossible to stop. Sensing her mental turmoil, he hugged her close.

"It'll all work out, El," he whispered against her hair.

Would it? And if not, where would it leave them? Hating each other? Wishing they'd never met?

She knew exactly where it would leave *her*. With a second bungled relationship.

This time, she initiated the kiss, tugging down his head, nipping his lip, his chin, mating with his tongue. Devouring.

Of all the people she had to fall for, she hadn't predicted him.

She hadn't predicted losing her heart.

Chapter Twelve

J.D. lounged in his room at the inn looking for a movie channel, when his cell rang. After returning from Ella's cozy home he hadn't been able to settle into sleep.

The clock radio on the nightstand indicated it was past eleven. An hour since he'd kissed off her lips—no, *she'd* kissed off *his* lips—at her door and he'd reluctantly left the warmth of her arms to step into another biting winter night.

Argh. He had not wanted to leave her house. He had not wanted to walk away from the peace and quiet and restfulness he felt in her home, in her presence. He'd talked about his cabin offering those amenities, but her home, her little brick-and-mortar Cape Cod with its grand, snow-laden weeping birch in the front yard, its three-foot stone wall bordering the sidewalk…

When had he felt so at home in a dwelling? His dad's house across the back alley, the apartments and condos where he'd lived in the ensuing years—none had the same effect.

He'd always believed his Vermont cabin was the place to restore his mind. Now he realized structure had nothing to do with contentment. It was the people inside.

Reaching across the sheets to the nightstand, he snatched up the cell before checking caller ID, hoping for her voice. "Hello?"

"Hey, J.D. It's Marty Hoskins."

His cottage caretaker. "Marty," he said surprised. "What's up?"

The old man got right to the point. "All this snow we been havin'? Dumped a pile on the porch roof of the cottage, caved in the west end. First saw it when I took a run by this evenin'."

"Any damage to the building?"

"None that I could see. Porch roof will need some fixin', but nuthin' that can't be done in a day or two."

"Thanks, buddy. Listen, I plan on coming Friday. Could it be repaired by then?"

"Oh, hell, yeah. Like I said, ain't nuthin' major. You want the old lady to get in some groceries?"

"If Miss Agnes wouldn't mind." J.D. smiled, knowing respect and good manners plus a nice check in the mail would get the old pair to do almost anything for him. He'd lucked out with the Hoskins living five minutes down the wooded country road.

"Nah," Marty said, "she'd be tickled. An' she'll clean

out the perishables when you leave, give the fridge a scrub-down."

"Thanks, appreciate it. I'll drop by with the check on the way home around five on Sunday."

"That'd be good, J.D. Me'n the old lady'll be glad to see ya."

J.D.'s mouth tweaked as he flipped the phone shut. The cottage would be warm, the roads plowed and the fridge stocked when he took Ella there in a few days. And he was taking her. Somehow he had to convince her to take the trip with him, *to take a chance* on him.

He scrubbed a hand down his face. Take a chance on him? *Jeez.* He was here to do a job, then it was back to New York.

Except you gave her a different impression when you mentioned long-distance relationships. Admit it, J.D. She's not like other women. You've known that from the start. She's done something to you no one has before. She's caught your heart.

Agitated by his thoughts, he clicked off the TV. He needed to *do* something, go for a run. A long, hard run. Which, of course, was out of the question considering the tenderness he still felt in his knee. Besides, she'd have his hide tacked to a wall if he strained the healing process too soon by loping six to ten miles around Walnut River.

Snatching his scuffed-leather bomber from the closet, he headed out of the inn. He'd take the rental and go for a drive, maybe grab a coffee at some hole-in-the-wall diner.

Forty minutes later, after circling downtown three times, sans coffee, he drove down Cedar Avenue, past her house where—yes, dammit—he had wanted to go from the get-go.

Her front windows were dark, so he took the corner and came up the rear alley. No lights anywhere. She had gone to bed.

Where he should go as well. But he couldn't. Not just yet.

He gazed through the silhouetted trees and wondered what it was about her that had him in this state, the one in which he was practically stalking a woman?

Irritated, he tapped restless fingers on the steering wheel.

Rule was, he took women out, had a pleasant time, took them to bed. He never gazed moonstruck at their windows. And he sure as hell didn't wish for a night of snuggling or for kisses at dawn.

Over the years he'd had two real relationships, if seeing the same woman for three months was real.

In either case, the urge to stay in her bed until morning, to—God help him—*settle down* had never entered the picture.

But, looking at Ella's warm little house…

Crazy visions formed.

Him sitting at her kitchen table, eating a plate of eggs and drinking coffee while they went over their daily schedules…watching TV with her cuddled in his arms on the sofa…him grilling steaks in the backyard…his dad walking over to join them, teasing their little girl with her dark eyes and chocolate hair—

"Jesus, man," J.D. muttered when an icy rinse of adrenaline crossed his skin. "You. Have. Lost. It."

Booting the gas, he drove out of the alley, sped back to the inn, hurried into the privacy of his room.

Where for the remainder of the night images of Ella zipped in and out of his dreams.

At seven-ten the next morning he sat at one of the tables in the inn's country kitchen. Greta, the female half of the proprietors, baked her pies at five and the scent of apple and cinnamon permeated the warmth of the room.

"How are you this a.m., J.D.?" she inquired, as a warning for him to move the copy of the morning's *Walnut River Courier* so she could set down his order of poached eggs and bacon.

"Very well, thanks, Greta." He placed the paper on an adjacent chair. "I'll need to double my workout when I get back to New York after all this food." He tossed her a charming grin and picked up his coffee. "No offense."

Pleased with his praise, she laughed. "None taken. I like my customers enjoying my kitchen." She filled his coffee cup. "You see this morning's article about the hospital?"

"Not yet." Though he'd caught the headline.

"Well, then. I'll leave you to read it while I run uptown to get a couple trays of muffins from Prudy's." She eyed him a moment. "I hope you'll come back and visit us often, J.D. But more than that, I hope you like our hospital."

He glanced up. "What makes you think I don't?"

She offered a small smile. "Your eggs are getting cold."

Small towns, he thought. *Your business is everyone's business.*

He reopened the paper. On page three Ella and Peter,

in blue scrubs and lab coats, stood in front of Walnut
River General's E.R.

*Our Hospital Treats Patients With Old-fashioned
Kindness* marched across the top in inch-high lettering.
The quote was one Ella had given. Biting into a strip of
bacon, he began to read.

Walnut River General is a hospital with history—
and a profound legacy. Established in the fifties, it
has had growing pains like any institution, but one
constant over the decades is its standard of compassionate, old-fashioned patient care.

'At Walnut River General patients are not numbers,'
explains Dr. Ella Wilder, the hospital's newest
orthopedic surgeon and the youngest daughter of
the late Dr. James Wilder, whose legacy of treatment extended beyond the city limits. 'Patients here
are treated with compassion and decency. They
aren't ushered in like cattle and sent home with a
bottle of pills that may or may not work. Yes,
Walnut River has a process we take pride in. It's a
process that understands human suffering.'

Fascinated, J.D. read the three columns. Both Ella and
Peter spoke of their father's beliefs, the policies and guide-
lines and standards James Wilder had instilled over four
decades of doctoring and, more recently, as chief of staff.

According to Ella, the reporter wrote, James Wilder
was sometimes considered archaic in his methods by
younger, ambitious medical staff. So she asked:

'If *you* were the patient, how would you choose to be treated, as a procedure or a person? What kind of bedside manner would you want your doctors and nurses to display: abrupt, hurried and indifferent, or friendly, kind and interested?'

Without thinking, J.D. checked off the latter. He'd been the receiving end of that *old-fashioned* doctoring and it had comforted him more than he wanted to admit.

During the past ten days, he'd wandered through the hospital talking to staff who gave him a jaundiced eye because he was the *enemy*. Oh, yes, he'd heard the grumblings in the cafeteria, the solarium, the corridors and around the nurses' stations—when people weren't always aware he stood a few feet away.

Rumors flew concerning fraud investigations incited by him in order to manipulate the hospital to bow to NHC whims, that his claim of gathering information for NHC was a ploy to dig its company claws into the tender neck of the small hospital. And in a sense they were right. But damn it…

He hated the way staff looked at him when he walked by. He hated how he felt when Frank Sorenson, his boss, sent BlackBerry messages with underlying currents: *Do what you have to. Document everything.*

J.D. couldn't deny the promotion, and its substantial financial bonus that had initially spurred him to take on schmoozing WRG's directors and medical echelon. But after seven years of working as Sorenson's right hand, he'd hit a wall of stagnation. Then, a month ago, his boss

offered the carrot, the means to get another foothold on
the mountain of success: *Get this deal in the bag and the
next promotion is yours.* Chief Executive. One rung
under Sorenson.

J.D. had always liked his boss, but in the past he'd
begun to question the man's ethics, his loyalty. Incidents
had cropped up that bothered J.D. The worst was the
laying off of Sorenson's secretary after New Year's.
Eighteen years the woman had worked for Frank before
the company decided her skills were no longer competent.

NHC had succinctly stripped the woman of a full
pension at twenty years in lieu of a young graduate
starting at a dirt-level wage.

The process stunk in J.D.'s opinion and, for the first
time since joining the corporation, he'd questioned his
own morals and ethics.

Ella's words in the *Courier* about legacies and old-
time philosophies gripped J.D. around the heart.

The methods she listed were those Pops had disclosed
the other day. They were the same methods J.D. wit-
nessed while under Ella's care. Even Greta implied there
was more to WRG than the outsider would ever see.

Outsiders like NHC. Like him.

Methods such as asking how a patient felt and what
s/he worried about at home made sense to J.D.

If the mind and spirit are in sync, the body has a better
chance at healing, Ella had been quoted as saying.

Further along in the article, she said:

'Comb their hair if they can't do it. Shave a man's
face if he's unable. Connect with your patient.

Put your heart into your work. People think doctors have god complexes, and some do. But at Walnut River General these simple tasks keep us grounded.'

He couldn't agree more.

Leaving the paper and his half-eaten breakfast, he returned to his room to make a few calls. The last was to his father. J.D. had a few things he wanted to discuss with the old man.

"Ella, wait up a second."

Her brother's voice had her pausing at the doors to the stairwell. "Morning, Peter," she greeted. "Can you walk with me? I'm starting my rounds and still need to stop off at my locker."

"Have you seen the paper yet?" he asked as they started for the change room. "The article's great, by the way. Wish Dad could be here to read it. It does him honor."

She glanced his way. "It didn't sound too biased?"

"You said it honestly. 'Our hospital has heart.'" Smiling, he held the door open. "Bethany wants to frame the article and put it in the cafeteria where everyone can read it."

"Bethany's a sweetie."

Peter's mouth bowed. "She is."

Ella chuckled. "You are so gone over her I'm amazed you're not floating up and down these hallways. By the way, are you taking her anywhere special tonight?" It was, after all, Valentine's Day.

He grinned and Ella felt a twinge of envy. What would

it be like to have someone waiting to spend Valentine's with *her*? Would she ever know?

Okay, she had fallen in love with J.D., but she was also a realist. They would never be a couple and she'd never walk around with the ga-ga expression her brother got around Bethany.

"Earth calling Peter," she said, shoving into the locker rooms. "You wanted to talk to me?"

He blinked. "Right." Clearing his throat, he pushed his hands into the pockets of his lab coat and followed Ella to her locker. Thankfully the room stood empty.

"I want you to call Anna because you girls were always close," Peter began. "Tell her what's going on here with J. D. Sumner."

Fingers calm but cold, Ella twirled the lock's combination. The door sprang open. "And what's that?"

Peter sat on a change bench, elbows on knees. "You know when you're trying to make a logical assessment of a patient's condition, trying to pin the problem, and no matter how hard you try you know it's not going to be good? That's what I'm getting from Sumner." He looked up at Ella. "I don't like that he keeps prowling the hospital corridors. Or that he has Westfield's endorsement to do so. It's not in our best interest."

Time. She needed time to respond.

But when she tugged on the lab coat, clipped on her ID, retrieved her pager, closed her locker, she still had no answer, except to ask, "You think Anna can do something?" *Against J.D.?*

"Our sister has an excellent head for business. She'd

know how to handle Mr. Sumner." Peter rose. "We received another fraud claim. Where they're coming from is anyone's guess, but Bethany is wondering if it doesn't have something to do with NHC. It's only a matter of time before the state attorney general sends an investigator."

Ella stared at her brother. "You think J.D.'s at fault."

"I don't know." His eyes held hers. "Are you still seeing him?"

"Would it make a difference?"

He was silent, then said softly, "Watch out, Ella. People are taking a dim view of Mr. Sumner. You dating him might appear like you're fraternizing with the enemy."

"Is that what *you* think, Peter?"

"It's not what I think that's at stake here."

"I think it is." Pushing past him, she headed for the exit. "I'm late for my rounds."

"Talk to Anna, okay?" he called.

"I'll think about it." At the door, she graced him with a haughty look. "And Peter? Unless you have evidence placing J.D. in the driver's seat of those allegations, we are not having this conversation again."

J.D. frowned at the message on his BlackBerry. He'd been maneuvering through some of the physiotherapy exercises in his room when the cell phone beeped, indicating a text message.

Frank Sorenson wanted him to call ASAP. Frank seldom did phone conversations. He was an e-mail man.

J.D. hit three to speed dial his boss's office.

"The man I wanted to talk to," the senior executive boomed, as if he hadn't just texted two minutes ago. "How's your data compilation going?"

"I'll be submitting my report Monday, sir," J.D. said.

"Good, good. The quicker, the better. Now, we've got another project for you. Can you give us some info on James Wilder?"

J.D. hesitated. What did Sorenson want with Ella's father? "Only that he was a fine doctor and an honorable man."

Sorenson scoffed. "No man's an island, J.D. We all know that. Dig up some dirt on him. Depending on the caliber of info, it could be a couple grand for you, plus a couple of extra letters after your name."

Forcibly, J.D. kept his muscles relaxed. "What's the plan, sir?"

"Company echelon wants that hospital. We just bought the Connecticut and Vermont ventures this week, and we want Walnut River General to make the trio complete for this year's budget."

J.D. was familiar with the two rural hospitals NHC had promised to upgrade last summer. At the time, he'd thought the company had decided to bypass the takeovers of those medical centers. Instead, the corporation-take-all policy he'd believed advantageous for Walnut River General on the night he spoke to the board—and crashed on the steps—continued on.

Suddenly, NHC looked like a voracious shark, eating everything and anything in its sight. He imagined Ella's face, the look in her eyes when she discovered how they wanted him to flatten the reputation of her late father—her hero.

"Why bother with James Wilder?" he asked mildly. As if his stomach wasn't twisting like a tornado.

Sorenson snickered. "He was the founder. Nothing like discrediting the founder. We've read the article in the *Walnut River Courier*, and the Wilders' attempt to appear wonderful, but we're also aware of the rumors floating around that hospital."

J.D. felt sick. "Who started those rumors? Our company?"

"Does it matter? They're out there and we want to capitalize on them, make the community think we'll be their saviors. Dig out James Wilder and his son is sure to follow." Another chuckle. "Like father, like son. Hell, make it a triple crown and toss in the daughter, too. Cover those bases and we're laughing all the way to—"

Lowering the phone, J.D. hauled in a breath. Sorenson wanted him to hurt Ella? The balloon of anger in his chest exploded into rage. *No way!*

"Frank," he said, bouncing a fist on his thigh. "Disgracing the family—its wrong." *Disgusting.* "Their whole lifestyle is medicine and helping the ill and injured. The people, the townsfolk know that."

"Give your head a shake, man. Remember the rumors? We don't want a public outcry. We want to be the good guys, the helping hand. You know how it goes."

Bastard. J.D. nearly threw the phone against the wall. "I do know how it goes, Frank, but you'll have to count me out."

"What did you say?"

"I said count me out."

"Are you saying—"

"Exactly."

There was a beat of silence. "You don't do this, J.D., you'll be writing your walking papers."

"Consider them written." He hung up the phone.

His stomach settled for the first time in almost a month.

At 5:45 p.m. that afternoon, she closed the door to her office, sank into her chair and shut her eyes.

Peter's conversation had nagged her all day—through her rounds, a three-and-a-half hour surgery, lunch with Molly, and a number of afternoon appointments.

She understood her brother's concern. It was why she'd done the article for the *Courier*. As much as Peter, she wanted their patients and families, as well as the town, to look upon Walnut River General as a committed, trustworthy, stable hospital.

And if Anna could help achieve that goal…

She dialed her sister's home number; heard it ring seven times before Anna's recorded voice cut in: *You've reached me. Speak your piece.* Which was so Anna. No frills.

"Hey, sis," Ella began after the beep. "Give me a call tonight, will you? I really need to talk about—"

"Ella," a breathless Anna greeted. "I heard the phone while I had the key in the door."

"Ah, heck. Sorry. I'll call back when you've wound down."

"No, no. Now's fine." A grunt and a soft thud drifted

across the line. "I just picked up some groceries for dinner. Nothing urgent. We can talk while I put the stuff in the fridge."

Rubbing her temple, Ella took a breath. "Okay. Here's the deal. Trouble is brewing at the hospital, and Peter thought you might be able to help us figure out what to do."

"What kind of trouble?"

"Allegations that we're not doing…a good enough job." She did not want to get into the details, especially Peter's accusation that J.D. might be involved. "The claims are escalating and we have no—"

"Before you go further," Anna interrupted. "I can't help you with that."

"Why not? You have business experience. You know the ins and outs of how corporations like NHC work. We need to know how to fight them, Anna. We need some advice and we don't know anyone who is more adept to—"

"Stop right there. I cannot help you. Get your board of directors to give you advice. Or the hospital administrator. I'm not employed by Walnut River General. I don't know the details, nor do I want to know them."

"This is Dad's hospital," Ella exclaimed. "WRG was his life. It's where you were born, Anna." And where she had gained a family—a family who loved her whether or not she believe it.

"I know whose hospital it is," her sister said quietly.

"Then help," Ella begged.

"I can't."

"Right," she bit out. "I'll pass on your enthusiasm to Peter."

"I'm sorry, El."

"Yeah. So am I."

"Don't be mad. It's truly nothing personal. It's just…"

"Sure. I understand. Nothing personal." She hung up.

Covering her face, Ella fought the sting of tears. *Oh, Anna. What's happened to you, to us? I don't understand it. Not at all.*

When her heart calmed, she prepared to go home. There she'd take a long, luxurious bath, then read a good book in bed. One day, maybe, she'd spend Valentine's night with someone special.

But not J.D. And not tonight.

Tonight she would return her dreams to that sheltered spot in her heart. And secure the lid.

Chapter Thirteen

J.D. knocked on his childhood home for the second time in a week.

"Son," Pops said, pulling open the door. "Thought you'd gone back to New Yawk."

"No, Pops, I didn't." He toed off his boots, walked through to the kitchen, breathed relief when he saw that his father was alone this morning. "I need to talk to you."

Jared limped after him. "Want some coffee?"

"No thanks. Pops, listen. I've been thinking of staying." He shot a glance at the old man. "What would you say to that?"

Jaw slack, Jared stared at him. "You wanna move back to Walnut River?"

"I was thinking of it."

The old man's eyes sharpened. "You planning on quittin' your job, then?"

"I don't know." *This is the first time I'm questioning the direction of my life.*

"Ah, I get it. You want me to tell you whether it's the right thing to do, that it?" Jared asked. As if he'd climbed into J.D.'s head and saw all his Johnny-come-lately confusion.

"Yeah, Pops. I suppose I am."

"Huh." The old man walked around the counter rubbing a hand over his scalp. He turned to J.D. "Can't, boy. Those choices you make yourself." From the fridge, he hauled a jug of water, drank deeply.

Frustrated, J.D. began to pace. Why had he thought he could discuss life decisions with his dad? Suddenly antsy to leave, he spun around and stared out the window at *her* house.

That's the problem, he thought.

He wanted more than a long-distance relationship. He wanted an everyday one. He wanted to eat at her table, watch *Lost* with her, brush his teeth in her sink. He wanted common everyday events. With her, only her.

His dad hobbled to the counter, set down the jug. "New Yawk must be good for the gab," he said. "Ya talked more in the past week than you ever did growin' up."

"I learned from the best." Regret burned J.D.'s throat.

"Ain't proud of that," the old man said slowly. "Shoulda done better by you. A father does for his son."

J.D. frowned. "You did, Pops." He walked over to the fridge, took down a framed picture of himself in a blue softball uniform. "You hit fly balls for me that summer."

He'd been nine in the photo. Pops had taken it in the backyard because the coach, an absentminded drunk, had forgotten to give J.D. the date for the team photo.

Brushing the dust from the glass, he smiled. "You may not have taught me much about talking, but you taught me how to play first base." He returned the photo to its place of honor on the fridge, thought of the paraphernalia in his bedroom. "And a whole lot of other things. Seems I've been lugging around a barrel of woe-is-me when it comes to you. Did you know I used to pray for you to change, pray you'd be like Prudy's husband next door? He did things like picnics and summer vacations to the New Hampshire coast with his family."

"Prudy's husband used to hit her. Bad."

J.D. stared at his dad. "Jesus," he said quietly.

Jared lowered himself carefully onto a chair; shook his head. "Don't know why I said that. It's her private business."

"It stays in this room, Pops. You got my word."

The old man nodded. "You always were loyal to a fault." An impish gleam entered his eyes. "Except for the prayin'."

"I was stupid back then," J.D. conceded.

"You was a kid, son. Can't fault you for not seein' the whole picture. Lotsa times I didn't see the global picture, an' me a grown man." His shoulders lifted on a sigh. "Know why I put the fear of God into you 'bout hospitals? 'Cause my old man died in one. Your mother's parents died in another. She died there. Hospitals scared the hell outta me. Tainted my view about medicine."

J.D. shifted uncomfortably. "Dad, you don't need to explain."

"Yeah, I do. What I come to realize finally, wasn't the hospital causin' my people to die, but their conditions. Cancer, a car crash, liver disease." He paused. "An embolism."

Which strike like lightning, J.D. thought. "I always figured you blamed me for her death."

His dad's eyes filled with sorrow. "Ah, son. Not once. Not *once*. But I will say this. My attitude changed when you was five an' went a tad deaf with that ear infection. Didn't know that, did ya?" he asked when J.D. blinked. "Temperature shootin' over a hun'red. I damn near went crazy debatin' whether to take you in or not. Called Prudy next door. She wasn't a nurse, but she had four kids. Told me to get my ass down to the hospital *now*."

An edge of J.D.'s mouth curved. "Long story short, I'm here."

"Yeah," Jared said, returning the smile. "You are. Hospital pretty much saved your hearing." He rubbed his hip, nodded. "Truth is, son, I'd be one glad SOB if you lived in Walnut River again. But I'm leavin' that choice to you. All I ever wanted was for you to be healthy an' happy."

What every decent, loving parent wished for their kid.

J.D. looked away, took a hard breath. Pops loved him. It didn't get much more right than that.

After a long Friday at the hospital, Ella entered her kitchen, tossed her coat over the back of a chair and rolled her aching shoulders. With no break since Wednesday the previous week, she was ready to laze around the house in her slippers and pajamas for the next forty-eight hours drinking peppermint tea and snacking on dark, divine chocolate.

When the doorbell rang, she told Molly, "This better be a surprise limo to take me to a weekend spa or there's going to be some serious door slamming."

It was J.D. With a sunburst of Gerbera daisies.

Yellow, gold, orange, crimson, white, violet. Where had he obtained summer in the middle of winter?

And...were those MarieBelle chocolates?

"This," she said through a laugh, "is *so* much better than a spa."

"This," he replied, "is the beginning of a great Valentine's weekend." He leaned forward, touched his mouth to hers. "Ready to go away with me?" he whispered, hovering.

On a groan, she latched her arms around his neck, pulled him into the house, kicked the door shut and let herself fall into his taste.

The fact he held the bouquet and the chocolates and couldn't put his arms around her drove her wild. She was in control. Of her sexuality, of the heat passing between them. She was the pursuer, he the pursued.

"Well," he said when she finished and smiled up at him. "That's the best start to a weekend I've had in a helluva long time. Come to think of it, I don't ever remember that kind of wow factor."

Laughing, Ella eased her arms from around his neck. "Maybe it's time for a lot of firsts." *Especially in bed.* She wondered what he would think when the time came.

Not wanting to dwell on his reaction—or hers—she

took the bouquet and carried it into the kitchen to run the tap, fill a vase. "These are incredible. Thank you."

He set the chocolates on the counter. "They reminded me of you. Bright and quietly elegant. God, I can't believe I said that." He rubbed his nose. "Next I'll be spouting angsty poetry."

She set the vase in the middle of the table. "I love angsty poetry. Used to write reams of it a hundred years ago."

"Yeah?" Grinning, he caught her hands. "I figured you'd be recording biology stats and sketching frog entrails, not drawing hearts and writing love poems."

She lifted an eyebrow. "Why? Because I was the nerd who wore braces and glasses and had two left feet?"

He chuckled. "Ah. The duckling that grew into a swan. Doc, you do intrigue the hell out of me."

"Good." She disengaged from his hold and headed for her bedroom closet. "Let's go to Vermont where you can get intrigued some more."

"You mean where I can get you naked," he called after her.

"We'll see." She winked back at him, then shut the door to change from her work clothes into a pair of jeans and her favorite soft-knit sweater—the hue of a Valentine heart.

Apropos, she thought, checking the full-length mirror on the back of her door where her image showed a woman with respectable breasts and hips, and the sweater tinted her cheeks and lips rosy.

She pulled the clip from her hair, shook her head. At the result, she felt a spike of lust so sharp she almost groaned. Within hours, he would see her hair tousled this way, her face flushed, her breasts and stomach and legs and *everything*…naked.

And then he'd come to her, touch her, kiss her…and be her first.

He would make this her first Valentine night. What would he think? What would he say? Would he be happy, amazed, thrilled?

She'd heard that men got an incredible high when a woman was a virgin. When they could chart the map, so to speak, of unexplored regions, be the *very first one*.

Whether those stats were true for all men, Ella didn't know. Nor did she know how J.D. would react. Heck, she had no inkling how *she* would react. Maybe, after all was said and done, she'd do the Highland fling around his bed. Maybe she would laugh—or cry.

And if she did cry…

Let it be with happiness, not regret.

A million migrating bees in her stomach, she picked up her tote of necessities and flung open the door.

Vermont, she thought, *here we come. Virginity, here you go.*

They headed out of town with J.D. behind the wheel of her Yaris. After ten hours of work, fatigue lay in her bones and all she wanted was to relax.

She tried not to think of what lay ahead—in the bed of a Vermont cabin.

She couldn't stop the nerves, couldn't stop imagining his hands, those big hands dusted with dark auburn hair and easy on the steering wheel, traveling with that same ease over the itinerary of her body.

As the outskirts of Walnut River approached, she attempted to think of more mundane topics. Like her telephone conversation twenty minutes ago with Prudy about Molly's care. Hearing of Ella's trip, her neighbor had said it all. "It's long overdue, dear girl."

Long overdue. Prudy had no idea how those two words fluttered along Ella's nerves. *Truth is*, she mused, staring at the wispy snowflakes drifting into the car's headlights, *it's a decade overdue.*

J.D. glanced across the console. "If you need to catch a few z's, go ahead."

"Why, do I look that haggard?" she teased.

"You look gorgeous. That sweater is going to be my downfall. But you sighed, and when people sigh they're usually tired."

"I am a little," she admitted, though she was too restless to shut her eyes. "Nothing a cabin in the woods won't cure."

He chuckled, reached for her hand and kissed her knuckles. "I'm glad to offer it. You work too hard."

"It's my life," she said simply.

He held her hand on his thigh and she felt the power of its muscle beneath her palm. "I won't argue that," he said. "But even life likes a break now and again. It's called play."

Her lips curved. "Is that what we'll be doing? Playing?"

"Among other things."

"And where will we be playing?"

"Wherever you want. There are ten acres of mountain woods outside the cabin and eight hundred square feet of floor space inside. The playing field is yours for the choosing."

She leaned her head against the seat. "Sounds lovely."

He switched on the CD player; Sarah McLachlan crooned about remembering and not letting let life pass her by. Slow and sweet the song curled around Ella's heart. Years down the road, would J.D.'s memories of her be the same as hers of him?

Doesn't matter. Having sex with someone doesn't make him yours. It's just sex.

Except for one small difference…she was in love with the man.

And if he knew, he'd run for the hills. The whims and wiles of sex might not be her forte, but she wasn't so innocent as to think he'd appreciate changing a virgin to a nonvirgin, then having her declare them soul mates.

As they drove through the snowy night toward Vermont, her analytical mind tried to reason away her jitters. She was a woman, with a woman's needs and wants. Was that so awful?

You should've left your heart at home, Ella.

Her inner struggle followed her into a troubled sleep.

"Ella."

She felt something warm against her cheek—a hand—and pulled herself from the dream of J.D. telling her how to remove a fragment of leg bone in the O.R.

"We're here, honey. Wake up."

Blinking, she sat up…and stared at the cottage ahead with its porch light a warm salutation in the dark. The snow had stopped and they were parked in a plowed spot to the right of a roadway circle fronting the structure.

Ohhh, she thought studying the cottage. *How very perfect.*

"Come on," J.D. whispered, letting his fingers linger on her cheek. "Let's go inside and see what Marty's stocked in the fridge."

They climbed from the vehicle, J.D. taking her tote and his carry-on from the rear seat.

Hands in her coat pockets, Ella gazed at the night sky with its trillion stars and white disc of moon whose pale light brushed the ragged outline of the woods.

"It's…beautiful," she said. "And so quiet. It's been a long time since I've heard this kind of quiet." Again, she took in the sky. "Maybe never."

"It's more noisy in the summer. Bullfrogs won't quit mating."

Mating. A flush seared her cheeks as she surveyed her surroundings. She had come here to mate.

And she'd picked J.D. to be the one.

She came around the car, took his hand. "Let's go inside."

The cabin was exactly as he'd said: rustic, rough and quaint. The logs were weathered gray. Rag rugs covered the main portions of the hardwood floor. To the right was a kitchen of sorts—stove, fridge, counter, a few cupboards. In a left corner, a cushiony sofa, recliner and wooden rocker huddled around a stone fireplace.

Carrying her tote, boot heels thudding against the

wood, J.D. headed for a stairway in the rear. "Bathroom is behind the stairs. Bedroom's up in the loft. I'll take the couch."

He was taking the couch? He didn't want to sleep with her?

Ella hurried after him up the stairs. At the top, she stopped as he set her tote beside a king-sized bed decked in an Amish quilt. "You're sleeping down...down there?"

He turned. "I didn't bring you here to seduce you, Ella."

"You didn't?" She swallowed the surge of disappointment.

He walked to her slowly, lifted a hand to her hair, let it sift through his fingers. "Unless you want me to." His eyes seized hers.

"I do. More than anything." God, yes, more than *anything*. She would take one, two nights with him over no nights at all. Because soon he would be gone and soon this sizzle, this electricity between them would be eradicated under the stamp of work and reality.

His hand settled on her shoulder, his thumb stroking the lobe of her ear. "I want that, too. More than anything."

"Then what are we waiting for?"

"Aren't you hungry?"

"A little," she confessed. "But it can wait."

"We can eat first—"

She slipped her arms around his neck. "J.D., I've waited a long time for this."

"You have?" he asked with a little-boy grin while he traced her bottom lip with the possession of a man.

"More than you know." She stared at his chest, took

a breath. "But…" How to say *I'm a virgin*? "We need to go slow."

His grin was lazy. "Honey, I can do slow. Real slow. So slow you'll be weeping."

"J.D.… I'm…" *Oh, damn.* Now the time had come, she'd lost her ability to speak, to think, to act. Her throat tightened. Her eyes gripped his. Seconds passed. And passed. She fell into his soul.

"Ella," he whispered, trailing his finger along her jaw, down the line of her neck. "You are so fine, so very fine. And I think I've…"

"Yes?" A mere breath.

Dark and enigmatic, his eyes pleaded for her to understand.

"J.D., touch me. Please."

He leaned down, brushed his mouth on hers, dispersing miniscule embers along the way. "I need to tell you something," he said, lifting an inch from her eager mouth. "You…You are the first woman I've…cared for this way."

"In what way?" she tried to tease, though her heart tumbled.

"With serious intentions." His words trembled against her mouth; his fingers shook on her skin. "Ella, I've never felt like this."

And suddenly her nerves fled. "Me neither. And," she tried to joke, tried to giggle, "I've never done this before."

His eyes tugged her in, deeper and deeper still. Right where she wanted to be. "No?" he asked softly.

"I've never had sex." She couldn't look away from

those green, green eyes. "I'm a virgin, J.D. Isn't that the height of jokes? Me a physician, knowing the human body like my own hand, yet I'm a neophyte when it comes to knowing what it's like to have…have a man's…" She huffed a laugh. "I want you to be my first."

He set a finger against her lips, then cupped her face. "Let me tell you something, Ella Wilder. I've never been so honored. Never."

She was going to cry. He wasn't running. He wasn't angry or upset or making jokes. Instead, he engraved his words onto her heart, so that sixty years from now she would remember this instant.

"Kiss me, J.D.," she whispered. "Make me a woman."

Laughing, he swung her up in his arms. "Ah, sweetheart," he said, carrying her the ten feet to his lake-sized bed. "Before the night's done, you'll be more than a woman. You'll be mine."

Forever, she thought.

J.D. gently laid Ella on the old Amish quilt, raining kisses across the soft, delicate contours of her face. *Ella. Sweet Ella.*

His own joy stunned him. Not because she offered such a sacred part of herself—which in itself was beyond description—but because she was the woman he'd fallen for like a brick from a high rise. She shattered him with her touch, her look, her words.

He wanted this night to be right, incredibly right. Because she had waited a lifetime.

She had waited for *him.*

The notion set his hands trembling as he worked off their coats and boots, as he touched her face, brow, lips.

"Ella," his voice rasped. "You dazzle me."

She drew a finger around his mouth. "J.D., just kiss me."

He did. Kissed her and kissed her until they were rolling across the bed, until his flesh sang with the heat of her.

His hands found her skin beneath the sweater, traveled up, up to the curve of her breasts. He wondered if a man had touched her there. And then he wondered no more, because if he did he'd put a fist through a wall.

No man will ever touch you here, except me. The thought burned his mind. He needed to see her, all of her.

"Ella. I'm going to take off your clothes." His lungs labored to stay calm, his hands to relax. "We'll go slow, honey."

Her eyes were the sky at dusk. Full of mystery and secrets. "Do I get to take off yours?" she asked, and her innocence drove him wild.

He wanted to yell and laugh and jump on couches.

"Yes, and as fast or slow as you'd like. Except," he grinned down at her, "if you go too slow in certain areas, we may run into a little…problem."

Coyness adorned her mouth and suddenly she was Eve and Venus and Aphrodite and every woman since the dawn of time. "Then that's what I'll do," she said. "Go slow. I want you crazy for me."

He couldn't halt his shout of laughter or the streak of heat in his penis. "Babe, you've got me there already." Rolling with her, he brought her above him. "Sit up a little," he whispered, tugging her sweater upward. "Lift your arms."

Gently, slowly, he brought the garment over her head and drank in the sight of her. Breasts shaped to fit his hands.

"Ah, gorgeous," he said, rising to set his mouth over blue lace.

"*J.D.*" Her hands were in his hair, her lips against his scalp.

Lifting his head, he danced his tongue into her mouth. His fingers unlatched her bra, tossed it across the room. Two seconds later he'd shucked his own sweater, threw it in the same direction.

Warm skin to warm skin.

A nip in the crook of her neck, a nibble on her shoulder.

Her scent wrote a medley of music on his soul.

She was purity and carnality and he was drowning in all that was her.

"Ella," he murmured. Only her name. He could not say more, could not get his throat to expel what filled his heart.

He held her face between his hands, looked into her eyes; tried to say *You're the first.*

She ran a hand through his hair. "It's okay, J.D. I'm not afraid."

But I am, he thought. *I'm so damned afraid of what I feel for you, afraid that I might hurt you in the end.*

"Undress me," she whispered. "Please, J.D." Her eyes said she was done with the preliminaries. "I want you."

It was all he needed. "Hang on." He dragged them off the bed to stand on the multicolored mat.

Working off their clothes they bumped heads and hands. Promises to go slow evaporated. And when they were naked, he took her hands, kissed her knuckles—and looked. From the crown of her hair to the tips of her toes, his gaze meandered.

Her cheeks were flushed, her lips swollen from his kisses.

He winced inwardly at the slight beard burn on her chin and neck, on her breasts.

I've put my mark on her, he thought, wishing for a nonabrasive method, knowing what they were about to do would hurt her again.

"I'm going to make love to you now," he told her.

"Thank goodness." Mischief flickered across her mouth. "I thought you might change your mind, you were taking so long."

"I want the first time to be special for you." How to say the words: *I've never wanted a woman this much? I've never* needed *a woman this much? I've never loved....*

"It will be." She kissed his mouth, a feather's stroke. "Because you'll be right there with me."

Mercy. She could reduce him to a mass of nerves with just a phrase. He sat her on the bed. "I'm going to kiss you first," he said. "Everywhere."

Grabbing a pillow from the bed, he knelt on the rug.

"J.D., no." She clutched his arms, trying to raise him. "Your poor knee—"

"My knee is great. You have a healer's touch."

"But, it's only been two weeks. You'll aggravate it."

"Not for thirty seconds." And then he worked his

mouth down her body—breasts, belly, across her thighs. For all her bravado minutes ago, he sensed shyness when she kept her knees tight. Gently, he parted them. "Open for me, sweetheart."

"J.D. This isn't—"

"It's okay," he said. "Just relax, let yourself float." Cupping her buttocks he brought her to his mouth.

"*J.D.* you're—"

And then her sounds were incoherent.

Later, he kissed his way back to her mouth. Her eyes were glazed. He smiled. "It's time, El."

"That was…J.D., I didn't know it could feel so *good*."

"I know. It gets even better." Reaching for his jeans, he dug the condoms from a hip pocket.

"Let me," she said, tearing a packet open. "Wow." She stared down at him. "You're—*amazing*." Shyness had prevented her from looking before, from touching. And it made him stiff as stone.

"Hurry, babe. Or I won't make it if you keep staring that way."

Quickly, she sheathed him. "Next time, I'm touching for a long time. And kissing."

He released a guttural groan. "Be my guest." And then he pulled her down, shifted her so she was beneath him.

"Wrap your legs around my waist, Ella," he whispered, sweeping her hands above her head. "It'll hurt a bit, but only once."

"I am a doctor, J.D. I know."

But she hadn't experienced it, hadn't felt the sting. And it scared the hell out of him. Because as much as he knew about climbing between the sheets with women, this was a first.

"I'll go easy as I can," he said, misery ruling his smile.

"I trust you."

Trust. Sweat struck his skin. Could she trust him? With this, yes. With her heart…?

He hoped.

"Try to relax, honey." Kissing her, he edged against her. His lips slipped across her mouth, cheeks, eyes.

And then he pressed. Sweat pebbled on his skin. His arms quivered to keep his weight light, the pressure gentle.

Abruptly, before he could decide his next move, she took command of his hips, towing him in with her legs until he felt her give, break. He heard her expel a breath and knew it was done.

Perspiration tickled his temples. Motionless, he let her body accept his, let her adjust to his strength, his size.

"Ella." His voice was sandpaper. His heart hurt with her discomfort. Words eluded him. All that was left was a sensation so powerful it swallowed him whole.

And then along her lips, came the sigh of his name. "Thank you," she whispered, stroking the hair from his brow and he saw tears leak from her eyes and drip to the pillow.

"I hurt you," he said, destroyed.

"No, J.D. You were wonderful. Gentle and tender and…I'll never forget this moment. Never, do you hear?"

He rested his forehead against her damp one, closed his eyes. *This moment.* When his body, his soul, brimmed with an emotion so unfamiliar it snagged his breath. An emotion very close to love.

No, not close. *There*. Right there in his heart.

Big and bold and true.

Kissing her mouth with utmost care, he let the physical govern, and take them to where he found release. To that *next time* when he could promise her pleasure and bliss and satisfaction and he could love her—the way a man did when he loved a woman.

Chapter Fourteen

Lying in J.D.'s arms, with the stars and the moon illuminating the cabin's window, Ella listened to his strong, steady heartbeat against her ear. Under her palm, his chest rose and fell in slumber.

He'd been so selfless and considerate this first time. She'd cried with the intensity of her feelings. He'd made it special for her. But then, *he* was special. He had read her reticence and coaxed her through it with kindness.

He was not a brash man, not flamboyant. He had a side she was just beginning to understand.

And she wanted him again.

In her mind, she compared her body with his. The softness of her calf as it lay over his bony shin. The crisp hair along that line of leg and across the expanse of his chest. The muscles in arms that held her tight to his side.

The quilt covered them, but she wanted to see him below. She wanted to explore him *there*, to know him *there*. Previously, the dark had hinted at potency, dimension, contour.

She wanted reality.

Slowly, her hand crept downward, over the plane of his abs, the dip of his navel, and—*oh, my.*

He was ready again. Very ready.

"Hunting for treasure, babe?"

Her head snapped up at the sound of his deep voice. Amused eyes looked down at her.

"I…wanted to…" *Do it again. Do you again.*

The moonlight showed the arc of one dark brow.

"I want the covers off," she said brazenly.

A lazy smile. "To have a good long look?"

Relaxing, she grinned. "Absolutely."

"Well, then." He kicked down the quilt until they were both exposed and he lay beside her, Adonis in moonbeams. "Look your fill, honey. And whatever else you wish."

She wrapped her fingers around him—and bent her head.

"Aghhh…Ella…" One big hand dove under the hair at her nape, shaping her skull; the other fisted in the bedsheet. "Not fair," he hissed.

"You want me to stop?"

"No! *Yes*!" He hauled her onto the length of his body, grabbed the packet off the night table. Seconds later, he lifted his hips into the cradle of hers. "Hang on, honey. This is going to be one helluva ride."

"Finally," she said, the cells in her body crying out for him. "Make love to me, J.D. All night."

He did.

Huddled in his sweatshirt, she sat beside him on one of the two bar stools at the small kitchen island, savoring the strong Brazilian coffee he had brewed and the veggie omelet she'd prepared.

Decadent. That's how she felt this morning *after*.

As promised, J.D. had loved her until they'd fallen into an exhausted sleep around four. At ten they'd wakened with winter sunshine gilding the room.

"Do you come here often in the winter?" she asked.

His hair was deliciously rumpled, his chest bare. She saw the marks her nails had etched, marks she'd kissed in their shower together forty minutes ago.

He shook his head. "I use the cabin for fishing mostly. Moose Creek up the road has some great rainbow trout." A quick, smug smile. "Caught an eight-pounder last fall. Gave it to my caretakers."

"The people who stocked the fridge and fixed your porch roof?"

When he'd mentioned the snow damage while they cooked breakfast, she went onto the porch in her boots to examine the repairs.

J.D. had stormed outside, yelling, "What the hell are you doing, Ella? Don't you know you'll catch pneumonia walking around in nothing when it's ten-degree weather?"

"Nothing" meant his sweatshirt. And her boots.

He'd dragged her back into the warm cabin, stripped

off the shirt the instant they were on the welcome mat, and made love to her against the door. She'd broken apart in his arms.

Sipping her coffee, she saw him glance back at that same door, remembering. "Yeah," he said. "The Hoskins keep an eye on the place. Agnes likes to bake, so when she knows I'm coming she always has a basket of treats sitting on the coffee table."

Around the handle of the current basket a red bow with tiny white hearts had been knotted. A Valentine gift. The thought of other women, other treat baskets, *other gifts*, stung her cheeks like a slap.

With her steady-scalpel hands, she spread jelly on her toast. "Do you usually bring women here?" she asked casually.

Long moments ticked by. He lifted his coffee, but didn't drink. "Worried you're one in a long line?" In his voice lay an edge of annoyance.

"Who you bring here, J.D., is your business."

"Yes, it is. But for the record—*and* to set your mind at ease—no, I don't bring women here. You're the first." He popped a bite of omelet into his mouth, chewed and swallowed. "And to further the record, I don't plan on bringing another. You'll be the last."

"That sounds ominous." She didn't like the direction of the conversation. Why had she even asked?

Because after all they'd done in the bedroom, she had insecurities about herself.

And then he took the fork out of her hand, laid it along

her plate. "Ella." He rotated the stool so that she faced him, knees between his thighs. "Look at me."

She lifted her gaze, clung.

"Do you honestly think I could have another woman in that bed after last night?" His hands drifted to her bare thighs. "Hmm?"

Her breath stopped. His fingers had inched upward. He leaned forward to nip at her mouth. "Answer me, Doc."

"I was…hoping not." Was that her voice, that hoarse whisper?

"Don't hope." His tongue tangoed along hers, while under the hem of the shirt his thumbs danced their own tango. "Just know."

Needing some fresh air, they drove to a hamlet nestled in a small valley of Vermont's Taconic Mountains where they strolled the streets, peeked in quaint boutiques and antique shops, had lunch at a mom-and-pop diner and drank steaming cappuccinos in a Victorian coffee house—and Ella understood the reason J.D. had bought his cabin in the woods. The ambiance, the leisurely way of the people cloaked her in a charming trance she wished could go on forever…. And then, before heading home, he steered her to one last shop.

"Hey, Ingrid," he said to the grandmotherly lady sitting with knitting on her knees. "Got that pendant?"

"Sure do." The old gal climbed to her feet, went to the counter, reached down to a shelf. "Can't believe you re-membered it." She smiled at Ella. "He called this morning, asked if I still had a necklace that caught his eye last October."

J.D. winked. "Couldn't believe she hadn't sold it."

Ingrid's eyes went soft as she handed over the velvet box. "Sometimes things just need the right owner."

Ella gasped when he lifted the lid. "Oh, J.D...." The tiniest star, moon and sun hung on a gold filigree chain.

"Thought you'd like it. Turn," he instructed, before his fingers brushed her nape and he hooked the necklace.

Facing him, she touched the delicate charms where they lay above the scoop of her sweater. "Thank you," she whispered.

He bent to touch his lips to hers. "You are my solar system."

The action, the words snagged her heart so hard she couldn't think or speak. She knew then she'd fallen into that rare, forever-love described in books.

Behind the counter, Ingrid sighed dreamily. "Yessiree. The right owner."

Ella waited as J.D. settled the purchase, then slipped her hand in his as they left the shop and walked to the car. Still, she couldn't speak. Last night she believed he'd given her a forever moment, and he had, but back in that shop... He had uncovered his heart.

Dusk was sliding down the mountains and snowflakes floated from the sky by the time he pulled in front of the cabin and shut off the engine. "J.D.," she murmured, looping her arms around his neck. "I'll cherish your gift always."

And then she kissed him...until the confines of the car frustrated both, and she climbed over the console into his lap as he shot the seat back into a reclining position, and her long woolen skirt was hoisted, his jeans opened, and flesh met flesh…until the windows fogged over.

The coupling left them both panting. He pushed back the hair from her eyes and framed her face to hold her in place. "I've never given a gift to a woman." His voice was like the night, deep and still. "Pops never had a woman to the house. Except for Prudy the neighbor lady, I didn't have a clue how to act around them when I was growing up. I think when he lost my mother, he went into a shell. When I was a kid he told me he wouldn't marry again because he didn't want to chance losing another wife in a hospital."

"No wonder you were apprehensive during your stay in ours."

He chuckled. "You got that, did you?"

"I did."

A soft kiss touched her nose. "You're a talented surgeon, Ella. You've made me see things I've been blind to."

"Not blind, just a little skewed perhaps."

"Perhaps." He curved her hair behind her ears. "My mother's dying tainted my perception of the medical system. She's why I joined NHC, why I went looking for answers."

"And did you find them?"

"Sort of. Actually, I found I don't need answers. I just need to understand." He gazed into her face. "Most of my life I've carried a big chunk of antipathy. And I'm not laying blame because at a certain age a person is liable for the choices he's made. But then you came along with your big dark eyes, your insatiable need to help. You took the bitterness away, healed it."

"You healed yourself, J.D." She traced his lips with her finger. "I'm not nearly as strong as you think. Did you know I'm seeing a psychologist? That every minute I'm at the hospital I work to gain back a piece of my confidence?"

In the quiet solitude of the car, and hugged by his body, she felt safe and intimate with her secret.

"Two years ago while I was still an intern, I operated on a five-year-old boy who had broken an ankle falling off a pony. The surgery was straightforward, no complications. Except I hadn't realized one of the nurses had gone on an all-night drinking binge and—" a shaky sigh escaped "—she didn't sterilize the instruments properly. The child almost died of blood poisoning. I nearly quit my residency over the whole thing, and to this day I can't look at an instrument tray and not see the parents' expressions, or Joey's white little face."

She swiped at the tears that persisted to wet her cheeks even after twenty-six months.

"Aw, baby…" J.D. stroked her hair, rubbed her shoulder. "I'm so sorry you had to go through that."

"He was so little, J.D."

"I know."

"Now you'll really hate hospitals."

He cupped her face. "Things happen, honey. In every job. I've come to realize that. You are an exceptional surgeon. Trust me on this, okay?"

Trust me. Yes, telling him had been a boulder rolling off her chest. She pressed her face into the warmth of his neck where the scent of him conveyed a comfort she could not explain.

"I've never told anyone," she whispered and felt him kiss her hair and wrap her tighter against his chest. She thought she heard the words, those prized words: *I love you.* Or had it been *Let me love you…?* She wasn't sure.

He kissed away her tears, kissed her—until they both shook for another reason.

She stood at the front door waiting for J.D. to check the cabin one last time, turning down the heat, closing the fireplace flue, and a pang of yearning went through Ella.

For the past two days they had lived in seclusion, made love everywhere. In the shower, against the door, on the kitchen stool, in front of the fireplace. And the past two nights in the loft—

Don't think, she told herself. *Don't think of never coming back.*

Truth was, since waking this morning her heart had hurt with the knowledge that today they'd leave this cozy idyllic home away from home. If she were any other person, she could live comfortably here for the rest of her life. With J.D.

But she was a doctor, he a businessman.

And they had other lives.

He strode toward her. Was he feeling the same bitter-sweet loss?

"We'll be back, El," he said, shouldering her tote. He leaned in, kissed her lightly. "I promise."

His declaration didn't detract from her sense of *never again*. She gave him a smile, went out the door.

Outside, a light wind swept snow off the porch roof, creating a cascade of glittering fairy dust across the steps, where they would leave their footprints, walking away.

Night had fallen when they hit the main highway back to Massachusetts. Ella leaned back in the seat and sighed. Tomorrow she'd be in the O.R. The thought sent a trill of excitement through her stomach. The hospital was her life and, she had to admit, more real than a weekend in Vermont.

But Vermont could be your life, too.

That depended on J.D.

She straightened. *Depended on J.D.?*

Was she that emotionally deprived she couldn't choose to have a good time without the man at her side?

Except J.D. was the one she wanted there.

His deep voice broke through her rumination. "I heard your brother's having the library rechristened in honor of your father."

The dashboard limned his cheeks, his strong jaw and the curve of that mouth—which had kissed her everywhere, which had made her cry his name over and over.

"Yes, at the end of the month," she said. "My father worked his entire life to make the hospital the kind of place where care comes first for the patients. He deserves the honor."

"He does," J.D. agreed. "It's too bad it wasn't done before he died."

"I know. But no one expected him to have a…" *Heart attack*. She could barely say the words nearly two months later. She pushed back a cuticle. "He'd been such a force for years. I miss him. A lot. He was my hero."

"Wish I could have known him."

She gusted a small laugh. "He would've been very hard on you."

"Why's that?"

"He was very protective of his family."

"And I wouldn't have measured up."

"Only because you are a man interested in his daughter."

J.D. shot her a look. "Good." He focused back on the road. In the headlights snowflakes spiraled toward them. "I like a man who looks out for his family."

"After the library dedication, Peter's hosting a cocktail party at his house for friends and family. Would you like to come with me?"

"Will Peter be okay having an NHC man in his home?"

"If he doesn't then I won't go."

"Ella, I'm honored, but you should be there, regardless. It's for your father."

"I want you there," she said stubbornly. "Peter will just have to accept that."

J.D. took her hand, held it on his thigh. "I'll be leaving soon, El. Tomorrow, actually. But I'll be back for the party."

Gooseflesh ran over her arms. "I see," she said slowly, thankful the dark hid her pinched lips. "Then this was the end?"

"End?" The word held a frown. "Not on your life. I may be going back to New York, but you and I will have—"

"How, J.D.?" she interrupted unhappily. "I come to your house one weekend, you come to mine the next? With the main item on the agenda concerning a bed?"

"Is that what you think we had? Just sex?"

She shook her head. "Weekend relationships won't leave a whole lot of time for much else." And just like that she felt something go out of the wonder of the last two days. He hadn't meant to be with her. Not in the way that it counted.

What do you expect? a voice grumbled. *He has a job to do.*

A job for NHC.

How could she forget? Vermont had put a rose-colored glint on the world, including her hopes.

Well, it was time to get back to reality. She tugged her purse into her lap and dug out her pager. There were three messages, one from the hospital and two from Rev. Blackwell. She frowned. The preacher never contacted her. Booting her cell phone, she sighed.

"Something wrong?" J.D. asked.

"Not sure." She clicked onto her voice mail. Blackwell's was the only call. Would she call Mrs. Parker? The old gal was having trouble with her hips and couldn't get out of bed. Her granddaughter was worried the woman had taken a fall she wasn't eager to disclose.

Ella shut the phone. "Can you stop at a house on Maple Street when we get back to town? I need to check on a patient."

"House calls on your days off?"

"It's who I am, J.D."

Again he took her hand, this time bringing her fingertips to his lips. The warmth of his breath, his touch, lique-
fied her insides. "I wouldn't have you any other way, Doc."

As long as she fit into those eight days a month, give
or take her On Call weekend.

Biting her cheek, she turned her face to the darkened
side window and listened to the hum of snow tires on the
frozen pavement.

Leaving physiotherapy on the main floor, J.D. clutched
the two pages of exercises Ashley had outlined for the next
month and headed down the corridor for the bank of elevators that would take him up to the medical offices and Ella.

It was almost noon and he wanted to catch her before she
left on her lunch break and before he left for New York.

From another hallway, Peter Wilder swung into step
with J.D. "Got a minute?" the chief of staff asked. "I'd
like to talk to you in my office." He nodded to the elevator
bank. "Fourth floor."

"I'm heading up there anyway," J.D. said.

Peter eyed him as they waited for the car. "To see
my sister?"

"I'm going back to New York in a few minutes. Just
wanted to say goodbye."

The doors opened and they stepped in. "Heard you two
went to Vermont over the weekend."

J.D. breathed slowly. "We went to a cabin I own." He
looked straight at Peter. "To relax." He waited a moment.
"Not that it's any of your business, Dr. Wilder, but I care
about your sister. A lot."

"As much as you care about this hospital, I'll bet."

J.D. shook his head. "Guess I deserve that. Considering what NHC is after."

"Ah." Peter crossed his arms. "The truth comes out. Does Ella know?"

They reached the fourth floor. "Why don't we discuss it in your office?" J.D. said smoothly.

Ten seconds later, both men were enclosed in Peter's narrow office which was congested with an overflowing bookshelf and desk, and featured a view of the parking lot.

"Let's get to the heart of the matter, Mr. Sumner," Peter began as he sat behind his desk and J.D. chose a guest chair. "I'm not a fan of you or of NHC. I don't know what the hell you've been up to, wandering these corridors for the past couple weeks, nor do I care. But if you think I'm going to believe the bull you've been feeding Henry Weisfield about NHC possibly donating funds to a specialized unit, you're wrong." Clasping his hands on a pile of files, he leaned forward. "I think you've been here to get information to take back to your employer. Information they can twist and turn against us. Know why I think that?"

"I do." J.D. watched the other man sit back in astonishment. "I came here under the auspices that we— NHC—would encourage your hospital to integrate into our network of regional hospitals. In the past NHC has bought out other smaller hospitals—with their consent," he stipulated. "But during my stay at Walnut River General, I came to understand its uniqueness, and its place within the community." He paused to let that sink in. "What I didn't know—until four days ago—was that NHC isn't on the same page as I am, isn't committed to the same things."

"In other words," Peter muttered, "they break promises."

J.D. shrugged. He would not, could not, surmise what actually happened or tell Peter his assumptions.

The chief of staff studied him for a moment. "You're not new to the company, are you?"

"Correct. I've worked for them for seven years. Worked my ass off and climbed the corporate ladder. This was my first assignment as an executive. I was thrilled to get it."

"I just bet."

J.D. ignored the jibe. "However, when they began asking for information I couldn't obtain legitimately…" He sighed. "Anyway, I made it known I wasn't in favor, that I wanted out. They gave me an ultimatum. I had a job to do and if I wasn't prepared to do it the way they wanted, they'd find someone else."

Peter's eyes narrowed. "They fired you?"

"No," J.D. said. "I've decided to resign."

"That's pretty drastic, isn't it?"

J.D. rubbed his temple. "Probably. But this wasn't the only incident. There've been others over the years that have bothered me, things I don't want to get into, but suffice it to say, I didn't like what I was seeing or hearing."

"Ah. You grew a conscience."

"I've always had a conscience, Dr. Wilder," J.D. shot back.

A contrite expression crossed the man's face. "Sorry. That wasn't fair." His eyes softened. "Ella know?"

"I haven't told her."

"Will you?"

"Not until the ink's dry. I'm going back today for some face time with my boss before I hand him my papers." He looked hard at Peter. "Can you keep this confidential for now?"

The man across the desk dipped his chin. "Done." He steepled his hands, tapped his lips. "Any future plans?"

J.D. shrugged. "Might do a little fishing in Vermont till I figure out my life." And told Ella he loved her, that whatever goals he aspired to would never hit the mark without her.

Peter's eyes were somber. "Would you be willing to offer some tips as to how we get NHC's monkey off our backs?"

For the first time since his alarm went off this morning, the tension in J.D. dissolved. "Are you asking for my help?"

"I suppose I am." Peter nodded. "Off the record, of course."

"Of course. However, I won't malign the company."

"I'm not into smear campaigns, J.D."

J.D. No longer foe, yet not ally, but perhaps the initiation of a cautious friendship. "Got a pen and a piece of paper?"

He had to wait until she was between patients before the nurse—Beryl—slanted him a leery look and led him down the short hallway to Ella's office.

On par with her brother's, the room was small but held a touch of home. One wall hosted several watercolors of mountains, sunsets and flowers; on another she'd hung three sketches of Molly. Her desk was full, but organized; in a corner of the window a pair of sun-catchers dangled—a hummingbird and a cottage garden.

Ella sat behind her desk, her slim hand jotting notes in a file.

"Your visitor's here, Dr. Wilder," the nurse said.

"Send him in." She hadn't yet looked up.

Slipping his hands into his trouser pockets as the door closed behind him, J.D. looked down at the woman he needed in his life.

Today her hair was in a stubby ponytail. A black-banded watch peeked from the sleeve of her lab coat. He'd bet the pink Nikes were on her feet matching the ever-present pink stethoscope around her neck, its bell tucked into the coat's breast pocket. His gaze drifted to the strip of blue blouse with its V of pale skin he'd already tasted a hundred times, where his pendant hung.

God almighty. Not once in all his years had he thought he'd be standing in a dinky hospital office at thirty-six years old, humbled.

But that's what he was, pure and simple. Humbled.

By her.

Because all along, she had believed in him. Deep down in her core, she had believed in him. Believed he was a sincere and forthright person. Yes, in the beginning she'd had her doubts.

She'd questioned him, hesitated over his reasons,

argued about his intentions. But when the chips scattered to the wind, she'd been the one left standing with her hand out in welcome, in friendship and more. So much more.

That first night—*that first time*—in the cabin's bed had been proof.

First she'd offered her trust, then she'd offered her belief *in him* when she disclosed the secret of her fragile confidence as a doctor.

And so he stood watching her, a thousand thoughts traversing his mind. "Ella," he said, his voice gravel.

Her head jerked up. "J.D.," she exclaimed, glanced at the closed door. "I hadn't realized Beryl had shown you in."

Brushing at her bangs in a gesture he recognized as solely her, she came around the desk and, as natural as a homing pigeon, stepped into his arms.

He set his face to the crown of her hair. "God, you feel good. I've missed you."

Around a chuckle, she said, "Me, too. It's been twenty hours since—"

"You kissed me blind at your door?"

After their return from Vermont last night, he'd dropped her off at her home on Cedar Avenue before she sent him back to the inn.

He had stood quaking in his boots, believing she was breaking it off, because confusion rode his brain and he hadn't figured out exactly where his life would go, only that he wanted it with her.

They both needed a good night's sleep, she'd told him. Then she had cupped his cheeks and kissed him, hard and long—as if she needed to stamp him into her memories.

If she only knew…

A twitch began along his lips. "That a blush I see?"

Her hazelnut eyes were luminous. "Amazing, isn't it?" She tripped a finger along his jaw. "After everything we've done?"

He kissed her nose. "It's what I love about you, those blushes. Never stop."

A nickel's worth of seconds passed. Her eyes held his. "You've come to say goodbye."

"Not goodbye. I'll be back next week for the party."

He couldn't tell her yet he'd rebooked the inn for the night, and would be returning to Vermont to decide on his career and life's direction. That his goals had quieted.

Once he had everything shipshape, in order, planned out…*then* he'd tell her, come for her. And hope like hell she'd have him.

Slipping his hands into his pockets, he retreated a step. "Soon," he said, meaning it in the most literal sense.

She caught her elbows. Her smile trembled. "Keep safe."

"You, too." A last look, and then he opened the door and left her standing alone in her office.

Chapter Fifteen

Ella stared at the door J.D. had closed without a sound. If she were a teenager, she'd run after him.

But she was fifteen years too late for those elements of drama. Plus, drama had never been her calling. And in high school, she'd been too engrossed in looking at a piece of frog bowel under the microscope to bother fretting over a boy.

So, why are you now?

Because seeing J.D. again, knowing they were done stung her heart with a pain she hadn't thought existed. Of course he said he'd be here for the renaming of the library and they'd see each other again. But this *thing* between them? Done, finished. *Concluded here.*

And that desperate kiss last night? Done solely

because she hated grudges and icy walls between her and the people she loved.

The way it was between her and Anna.

So she told herself.

Right, Ella. Keep the friendship channel open. Easy, accessible and noncommittal.

Exactly what she needed—and he wanted.

Blinking back the burn in her eyes, she turned to check the schedule on her desk. Time for her next patient.

The next nine days were crazy. She had five major surgeries slotted, plus a weekend's rotation. Afraid she'd think too much about J.D. and the reasons he hadn't contacted her in a week-and-a-half, she returned to the hospital the following Wednesday—her day off—and fell into bed that night, exhausted. She'd been going flat-out from five each morning until nine each night.

She would not think of J.D.

She thought of him every spare second.

Thursday morning, the day of the hospital's library event and Peter's cocktail party, dawned bright and cold. She awoke as she had for the past three weeks with J.D. in the ebb of her dreams. She arrived at the hospital at five, did her rounds and was in her office at eight-fifty when her pager went off.

Simone Garner needed Ella down in the E.R. Ambulances had brought in two patients, an adult woman and a child. Both had been in a car crash five miles north of town on the same highway Ella and J.D. had traveled eleven days ago.

"The mother, Courtney Albright, is stable," Simone told Ella when she halted momentarily at the triage station to assess the information the paramedics recorded on the victims.

Ella's head came around. "Courtney from the gift shop?" Everyone in the building knew the single mother who managed the shop on the main floor.

"The same." Simone spoke in her practical no-nonsense voice. "It's not good, Ella. The car was small. Took the fire department an hour to get them out. We've got the child stabilized, though she took the brunt of the injuries."

Ella flipped open the chart. "X-rays?"

"Lab is sending them. But there's also…. Courtney is going a little crazy. The child's facial damage is quite severe. Possible broken cheek and jaw, nose and left wrist. Also a torn ear and one eye has a deep gouge at the corner."

"Poor little thing. Courtney?"

"Could have a mild concussion, and she's unable to move her left wrist. Very painful and twice the normal size."

"Likely a fracture. If it's swollen we'll have to wait to cast it. Where's Peter?"

"Trying to calm Courtney."

Ella glanced toward the E.R. "Which one?"

"Seven."

Chart in hand she headed for the room. Her brother stood talking to a young blond woman holding the hand of a tiny child under a lightweight blue blanket. Janie.

Nodding to Ella, Peter stepped aside. "Courtney," he said, "I've called Dr. Wilder in to assess your wrist and Janie's injuries. She'll know exactly what to do."

Ella understood he was trying to lessen the worry in the mother's eyes. With a smile she didn't feel, she went to the opposite side and looked down at the child. Thank God for medicine. Though her face was bloody, distended and bruised, the little girl was almost asleep with the medication dripping into her tiny veins from the IV pole.

"Hi, Janie," she said softly. "I'm Dr. Wilder. But if it's easier to remember, you can call me Dr. Ella." She'd found that a first name often put children more at ease.

Simone strode into the room. "Just in." She slapped the X-rays onto the viewers. Peter and Ella quickly surveyed the negatives.

"Janie." She returned to the bedside. "You've broken a little bone in your wrist, so once the swelling goes down I'll put a cast on it, okay? Let me guess your favorite color…pink?"

The child's battered lips tried to smile.

"Mine, too," Ella said, checking each tiny finger, the forearm and elbow where skin had been scraped. "One pink cast coming up. Now, I'm going to talk to Mommy and Dr. Peter for a minute, okay? We'll be right outside the door. Mom can hear if you call. You going to be a brave girl for her?"

"Mmm." The child's eyes blinked slowly.

"See you in a bit," Ella whispered.

In the corridor, Courtney turned on Ella. "What about her face? I don't want her face made worse than it is." Shaky fingers rubbed her forehead. "It was my fault, you know. I should have waited until tonight and gone after school instead of before. But they told us she was going to get an award as February's student and I wanted to celebrate before I went to work so she'd have something for Show and Tell this morning. God, why couldn't I have waited till tonight?"

Peter set a hand on the woman's shoulder. "Courtney, Janie will get the best possible care. We'll order several more scans and tests before we proceed. Right now, I need you in a bed. You could have a mild concussion."

"I can't leave her. I *won't* leave her." Full of despair and panic, her gaze darted between Peter and Ella. "I'll just have to wait." She drew in a hard breath. "This is awful. *Awful*." She glanced down the hallway. "I've been hearing things about the hospital and…and this corporation that wants to buy it, and—and—what if they close the gift shop? Oh, God." She pressed her fingertips against her eyes. "Who'll fix my baby's face? Her cheek is fractured, isn't it? That one X-ray…"

"Courtney, we—" Ella began.

"I can't afford a plastic surgeon. I just can't." Tears wet her cheeks as she looked at Ella. "Please… Tell me what to do."

"First off, let's concentrate on getting you fixed up so you can be there for Janie. Peter and I will decide who is best for your daughter's reconstructive surgery." She offered an encouraging smile. "She'll be in the best hands. Trust us on that. And we'll sort out the expenses as we go. Okay?"

Courtney glanced over her shoulder where Janie slept on the other side of the doorway. "I just want my baby to be normal again."

"She will be."

"She's all I have."

"I know." Ella's heart ached for the young mother. "We're going to take care of her. But she needs rest and to stay calm until the swelling goes down. Most of all, she needs her mom to stay calm."

Courtney sniffed, swiped her good wrist under her nose. "Okay. I can do that for her."

Gently, Ella touched the woman's shoulder. "Peter and I will be back in a little while."

They watched Courtney slip into the room again before they headed for the nurses' station. Ella said, "I want to call David." Their brother had a star-studded practice that put youth back into the faces of celebrities.

"He's in New York at a symposium."

"I know. Which means he's nice and close. No excuse. I want him to look at the girl, Peter. Maybe take on the case."

"And how is he going to do that, Ella? Have you forgotten he has a practice and patients in L.A.?"

"Who can afford to wait. Janie Albright can't. Besides, Courtney's worked in that gift shop on the main floor since she was twenty. She's been a part of this hospital for eight years. Always treated the staff and visitors with a smile. Even sends gifts to patients who have no visitors or family. Don't know how she finds out, but she does." Ella sighed. "I think we owe her one."

Peter nodded. "Can't argue that. All right. Give Dave a call." He started away. "And tell him since he'll be in town anyway, I'll expect him at the party tonight. Might as well do two birds with one stone."

Ella grinned. "I'll tell him he can stay with me tonight."

Peter's eyebrows rose. "Won't that be a little cramped? I thought J.D. was coming to the party."

Hearing his name, she felt her heart kick. "Even if he is, what makes you think he'd be staying at my house?"

Peter grinned. "Uh-oh. Trouble in paradise already?"

"Don't you wish."

"Actually, what I wish is for you to be happy, El."

"Who said I'm not happy?"

Peter simply looked at her. "You've been wandering around this place like the Tin Man from Oz."

"I've been crazy busy."

He chucked her under the chin. "Tell it to someone who doesn't know you. Get back to me on David."

Ella watched Peter walk away. Had her heavy heart been so visible? Nine days J.D. had been gone and she hadn't received a phone call or an e-mail. Nada. It was as if he'd never touched her.

Except he had. He'd done more than touch her life; he'd been in it completely—*in her*—for two nights and two days.

And then he had done what she had hoped, had prayed, he would not do. He'd walked away and not looked back.

He hadn't called to let her know he wasn't coming. With a smile that ached with every hour, she'd watched and waited through the rechristening ceremony at the hospital, through dinner with Peter, Bethany and David, and now at Peter's cocktail party.

J.D. had stood her up.

Should she be surprised? He'd made it clear he hadn't wanted a real relationship with her. What made her think his promise to show up for a party—to which he would need to fly—would have him back in her arms?

He'd gotten what he wanted.

With a bonus.

What a fool she'd been. Her virginity and her vulnerability. All in a single weekend. *Dumb, dumb, dumb, Ella.*

"So, sis, are you enjoying doctoring as much as you hoped?"

David came beside her as she stood, wine in hand, staring out the living room window where snow dusted the street lamps' luminosity.

"Loving every second. Hmm, don't you look handsome tonight?" Her gaze zoomed over his tailored charcoal suit, the crisp white shirt.

He chortled. "You know, if you weren't my sister I'd think you were hitting on me."

"And it's nice to know your ego hasn't diminished. Have you decided to take the Albright case?"

He sipped his beer. Her brothers had always preferred beer to wine. "It's…complicated."

"I'm sure it is," she said, thinking of the girl's face. "Well, I know you'll make the right decision, one way or the other. How was Courtney when you did your consult?"

"Won't leave the girl's side. Which is understandable." He gave Ella a sideways look. "Does she have a problem with doctors or men in general?"

"Not that I know of. Why?"

"Just some comments she made." He lifted his beer, sipped. "Thinks I'm some hotshot, golf-playing face-lifter in lala land."

Ella laughed. "Can you blame her? You're a handsome man—even for a brother. And you doctor the rich and fabulous."

He grunted. "Don't know if I should be pleased or not by that."

"Oh, you'll sleep tonight, trust me." She grinned. "Incidentally, you're staying at my house, right?"

"Nope." He flicked at her hair. "Just to evade your scorn, li'l sis, I've booked into the Walnut River Inn."

The place J.D. had lived for almost a month. Before he vanished from her life. She shook off her melancholy. *Don't be a whine, Ella. Get on with life.*

And that's when she saw him. He'd come into the foyer, long black trench to his boots. His eyes caught hers, held. "Excuse me," she said to her brother.

Wending her way through the crowded living room toward him, her heart skipped.

"Hey," she said, unable to hold back her smile.

"God, you look good enough to eat," he murmured, leaning forward a few inches as if to inhale her scent. "That little number…Jeez, Ella. Do you have any idea what that shade of gold does to your eyes and skin?"

She gave him a coy smile. "Possibly." The dress she'd bought with him in mind—and those Gerbera daisies he'd given her for Valentine's Day.

He groaned softly. "Listen, honey. Sorry I'm late. Flight was delayed because of deicing."

Yet David's plane had no problem with ice. Had the weather changed within hours in New York?

Shoving her mental debate aside, she stepped up and gave him a hug. "I'm glad you're here," she said, motioning for him to hang his coat in the closet.

A few minutes later she led him into the crowd, introducing him around to those who hadn't met him before, including David. Peter and Bethany caught up to them there.

"J.D.," her eldest brother said, offering a hand, surprising Ella with the gesture and the friendly smile. "Good to see you made it."

Ella's shoulders relaxed. He had come, he held her hand, he looked at her with those intimate eyes.

An hour passed. To J.D., she said, "I need water. Want some?"

He held up his beer, grinned. "Still working on this."

She squeezed his hand, then headed for the kitchen. There, dozens of people munched on finger food arranged on counters, and chatted in pairs or small groups.

What is it about kitchens? she mused weaving her way to the fridge. No matter how many parties her parents had hosted, guests always gravitated to the kitchen, the hub of the home. Peter's house, with its dark wooden cupboards, offered the same warmth which Ella surmised was part of Bethany's touch.

Plucking a bottle from the shelf, she moved near the dining room entrance. At least sixty people milled throughout the house.

She recognized many. Physiotherapist Ashley chatted

with nurses June and Lindsey. Medic Mike O'Rourke stood in deep conversation with Simone Garner. At the large butcher-block island, Henry Weisfield loaded chicken wings on a paper plate. Among the guests, a waiter wielded trays of champagne and hors d'oeuvres. And then J.D. wandered into view, his tall frame placing him above most people, his chestnut hair igniting under the lights.

Two seconds later his eyes locked on her. He'd come seeking. She felt it in her bones. God, but she wished they were alone, that she could simply walk over, slip her arms over those sturdy shoulders and hold on forever.

Except for those few words at the door, they hadn't a chance to speak alone. She wanted to ask him a million questions, dole out a million kisses. She was sick with want and need and desire for him.

Somewhere music played, and she caught lyrical snatches about stories and rules being broken and she recognized Brandi Carlile, an artist she'd recently come to favor. The song burrowed into her heart while J.D. kept her immobile with a slow, secret smile, and she thought, *It's more intimate than a touch.*

Suddenly, a woman's words intruded. "…almost lost her medical license over it…" The speaker stood behind Ella, several feet inside the dining room.

"Really?" a man queried softly. "In Boston?"

"Yeah…dirty scalpel or something…should've checked…"

"…the little kid?"

"Lived, thank God."

More murmurs. The man said, "Heard she's a great doctor…."

"Yeah. Father was…"

A few feet in front of Ella a group laughed, drowning the name, but she didn't need confirmation as to who held their interest.

Riveted where she stood, she let pain spin through her chest. *J.D.*, she thought, watching him cant his ear toward Henry Weisfield, who snagged his attention.

Why?

She had told only two people about those terrifying days following that Boston surgery. Her counselor and him. She'd talked her fool head off, *to him*. About the scrub nurse, about the days she'd waited, her insides churning, as the child's life wavered on the life-and-death fence. About her fragile confidence and the strides she had gained.

Easing away from the refrigerator, she turned enough to catch sight of the couple alone in the dining room. The man had his back to her, but the woman faced the kitchen. Ella recognized her as the young pediatric nurse she'd briefed three weeks ago about a six-year-old boy with a shattered elbow following an ice-skating tumble.

Why had the nurse been invited to the party? Clamping a vice on what could be nothing less than J.D.'s betrayal, she turned and walked into the dining room.

"Hello, Clarice," she said, watching the woman's mouth drop. "Having fun?"

"Y-yes. Thank you."

Ella smiled at the man, whom she recognized but couldn't place, likely Clarice's date.

Gossip, Ella knew, fed through the hospital corridors like grassfire. She said, "I overheard what you were telling your friend about an intern. For the record, Clarice, your information is completely incorrect. So. If I hear of it *anywhere* again, I will personally see that neither of you ever work in another medical facility." With a smile that hurt her cheeks, she left them to find J.D.

What the hell happened? he wondered.

Standing by the glass doors leading out to a vast back deck, J.D. waited as Ella pushed through the crowded kitchen.

"What's wrong?" he asked, the instant she grabbed his hand and began pulling him through the house.

Not a word and, except for those dark eyes flaying his hide when he asked, not even a look.

"Ella. What is it?"

She yanked her coat from the entrance closet. "We need to talk. Privately."

"O-kay." He was all for private. He'd wanted it for the past ninety minutes.

"Hey, you two." Peter strolled into the foyer, smile on his face. "Leaving so soon?"

She flung open the door. "I need some air."

"We'll be right back," J.D. said with a wink to ward off any red flags.

"Ahh." Peter chuckled. "Gotcha."

Outside on the front porch, the crisp February air streamed into J.D.'s lungs. "El—"

She wheeled on him. "Why did you take me to

Vermont, J.D.? Was it to lull me into submission, to—to find out a few dirty little secrets so you could use them to make Walnut River look like a bungling hospital staffed with inept doctors? All those rumors floating around about overbilling and the state medical examiner's office sending letters about fraud—was that you?"

He stared at her. "What the hell are you talking about?"

"Why haven't you called since you went back to New York?"

"Is that what this is about?"

"Not at all. Because I know why you didn't call. You didn't have the guts. But what really galls me is that you had the audacity to show up here tonight with that Mr. Innocent look on your face."

"Jeez, Ella." A frustrated hand drove through his hair. "Would you make sense, please?"

She stalked across the porch, its soft amber lamp outlining the delicate line of her brow and cheek. In the vee of her blouse, her pulse beat like tiny bellows, making the pendant he'd given her quiver.

"I had a conversation with a nurse two minutes ago," she hissed and he saw the angry sheen in her eyes. "*After* I overheard her talk about an intern operating with unclean tools that almost cost a child his life."

Stunned, J.D. blinked. "Did she mention names?"

Ella snorted. "She didn't have to. I heard enough to know *who* she was gossiping about. Do you know I've never told a single soul about that mistake? Not Peter, not even my father before he died. The only person who knew was my counselor in Springfield."

And him.

J.D. rocked back on his heels. "Ella, every conversation we had has stayed in here." He thumped his chest. "And here." He tapped his head. "My private life is not open for public forum."

"But mine is, that it?"

He shook his head. "Don't you get it? Yours became part of mine the moment you were my doctor in that E.R."

She stepped back, tears clouding her eyes. "Have a nice life at the top of that ambitious ladder, J.D." She spun away to hurry down the porch stairs.

"Ella!" He strode across the deck as quick as his knee would allow, but she was on the run to her car and within seconds disappeared around the hedge bordering Peter's front yard. *Dammit.* This was not how he pictured an end to the evening.

All day, he'd been impatient to return to Walnut River, to tell her his news. Hoping, praying she would accept his offer.

Down the street a car gunned and roared away.

Okay. If she needed time to cool down, he'd stay out of the way for a day or two. But he wouldn't wait forever. If she didn't come to him, he'd go after her.

One thing she would discover about him. He wasn't a guy easily swayed when things got edgy. Fact was, he thrived on edgy.

Oh, yeah. Anger smoldered in his chest.

Three strides and he pushed back through Peter's front door. Someone was smearing Ella's name and he was going to find that individual if it took all night.

Chapter Sixteen

One hand on the steering wheel, Ella swiped the tears wetting her cheeks. Such a idiot she'd been. Such a *stupid* idiot.

Instead of running, she should have forced him to leave. But no. Embarrassment had her stumbling like a drunk down the sidewalk to her car. She might have held it together, too, had she not spotted Simone Garner and Mike O'Rourke in a lip-lock across the street beside his vehicle.

God. That had been her with J.D. eleven days ago.

She had wanted to yell at Simone, *Don't let that kiss fool you! It doesn't mean a damn thing!* Instead, she'd jumped into her car and raced off like Danica Patrick at the Indy.

Swinging into her alley, Ella sought the little garage

beyond the headlights. Several minutes later, the warmth of her house wrapped her in a welcome cocoon.

"Hey, sweets," she said, bending to pick up Molly weaving between her ankles. "Want some cuddles?"

By the time Ella donned her pajamas and crawled under the covers, it was nine o'clock. The earliest she had gone to bed in years. Well, she would catch up on some of her reading.

She was midway through an article about shoulder arthroplasty in *The Journal of the American Medical Association* when her phone rang. Caller ID indicated Peter.

"Where'd you disappear tonight, El?" her brother asked.

"Sorry, Peter. I'm just tired."

"Nothing else going on?"

"Nothing that won't rectify itself."

A beat of silence. "Wish you could have stayed. After everybody left Dave, Beth and I had a great catch-up session. We missed you. And J.D.," he added.

"What is it with you and this *J.D.* stuff?" she scoffed. "Like you're friends all of a sudden." She sounded twelve, but she was past caring. "Anyway, he's gone back to New York."

Another pause. "Actually, he's staying at the Walnut River Inn with David. You guys have a spat, honey?"

Both her brothers always had been able to key into her emotional nuances. Not that she didn't appreciate their concern, but sometimes she wished they would simply butt out. "I don't want to talk about it."

"All right. But if you need any—"

"Fine," she blurted, her emotions surging like Mount

Saint Helen's. "You want to know? Here it is—you were right. I was a fool to get involved with him. The man's not to be trusted."

"Oh?"

"He broke a confidence," she cried, the hurt cutting her in two. "Something that happened to—to me a while back."

"Would this something concern Clarice Yves?"

Omigod. The woman had told the world. "What about her?" Ella snapped.

"J.D. and I had a chat with her tonight."

Ella's jaw dropped. "You what?"

"It's okay, El. We got it straightened out."

"What do you know?" she asked, suddenly drained.

"Not much. J.D. wouldn't say exactly, only that she was spreading unfounded gossip. He alerted me. We took her into my study and had a chat. Apparently, a friend of her mother's is a scrub nurse who worked with you in Boston."

"So, you know it all, then."

"Not the details. Seems the woman showed up today, unannounced, and wanted lunch with Clarice in the cafeteria."

"Convenient," Ella mocked.

"According to Clarice, the woman is bitter because she was fired. However, J.D. set the record straight about who was at fault in that O.R. when you were interning. Clarice will apologize to you first thing in the morning."

Ella sighed. "Yeah, well, the damage is done." *In more ways than one.*

"If you're worried about the guy she told, he's her boyfriend, a cop in North Adams. He worked the Albright crash."

Several moments passed. Ella took in what Peter had said, imagining the scene in his study. J.D. had gone back into the crowded house and sought out Clarice—and saved Ella's name. And what had she done? Called him a traitor and a liar.

"God, I've made such a mess of things."

"J.D.'s all right. So I'm beginning to discover."

"Make that two of us," she lamented, feeling sick.

"Oh, I hear you. I had my doubts at first. But when he told me he was resigning from NHC, I knew I'd pegged him wrong—"

"He *quit* NHC?"

"You didn't know? Oh, hell," Peter muttered.

"When?"

"You need to talk to him, Ella."

"When?"

"When he returned to New York. He told me the morning he left. We had a little, um, meeting before he went to see you. Apparently, he's been tying up loose ends this past week, even put his condo up for sale. He plans to move back here."

She was speechless. J.D. was moving to Walnut River? "Did he tell you why he resigned?"

"Only that he didn't like the way things were going with NHC."

Why hadn't he said something to *her,* given one tiny hint of his decision? Why had he left her guessing, wondering, waiting? And why hadn't he called her from New York? Why, why, *why*?

She couldn't stop the hurt that he'd shared such life-altering information with her brother but not her. Not even a clue last night.

And she'd spent almost two hours with him, smiling, chatting, listening, holding his hand. Breathing his scent. *Dying to kiss him.*

"You know," Peter interrupted the train wreck in her mind. "With Henry resigning as hospital administrator in a couple months, J.D. should consider applying. I think he'd be a damn fine replacement. You should put the bug in his ear."

"Yeah," she said, sapped of feeling. "Sure." *When I see him. If I see him.* "Good night, Peter."

"You going to be okay, El?"

"I'm fine." *Hunky-dory.* "See you in the morning."

Evidently he didn't want to let her go yet. He said, "The ceremony this afternoon was nice, don't you think?"

"Dad would've been proud."

"Yeah," he said. "He would've been. The James Wilder Library has a nice ring to it."

"He loved research and the hospital," Ella put in.

"Having your *Courier* article framed and hanging by the door was a great idea."

"Give Bethany a kiss for that. It was her idea."

"I will. 'Night, El."

After setting the receiver back, she sank into the pillows, a warm glow in her heart. The library had been upgraded with five hundred new books—and an honored name.

She couldn't wait to tell J.D.

That fast the warmth vanished, and a shiver took its place.

She had walked away from J.D., had shattered that special something between them with her distrust, her accusations.

"Oh, Molly," she murmured to the cat purring against her side. "What have I done?"

She rose at dawn, eager for new beginnings, for righting wrongs. All night she'd wrestled with worry that she would be too late, that he would be gone and her chance gone with it.

En route to the hospital, she planned to stop at the inn, rouse him from bed, argue if need be. Whatever it took, she had to convince him they could get through this. Failing that, she intended to strip off her clothes and seduce him.

She had to make him understand, make him see her error, beg forgiveness and a second chance.

At 5:35 a.m., bundled in her knee-length woolen coat, she picked up her briefcase and purse and stepped out onto her back porch.

Night still enveloped the world. Across the alley she saw that old Jared was up earlier than usual and had turned on the light above his back stoop, revealing a trillion snowflakes eddying out of the dark. A car—she was sure it was a taxi—drove slowly down the alley.

Suddenly a figure walked through the gate next to her garage and headed across her backyard toward the house.

Apprehension rushed through her veins. She hadn't

turned on her own porch light, but it wasn't difficult to see by the broad shoulders, the height, that it was a man.

Her fingers tightened on the briefcase. If he meant her harm, she would not go down without a dirty fight.

He approached steadily and suddenly there was something familiar about his shape and coat, that long, black boot-length coat.

"J.D.?" she whispered, one gloved hand reaching for support of the porch pillar.

He stopped a half-dozen paces from the bottom stair. "I was hoping you hadn't left." The deep tone of his voice sang in her heart.

"I was coming to see you," she said. "To the Inn."

"I'm no longer there. Checked out fifteen minutes ago."

A smile tugged her lips. "What are you doing here?"

"Don't you know?"

He hadn't moved, hadn't stepped forward. But hope soared anyway. And then she saw it, the suitcase. "You're leaving again."

"I'm leaving," he acknowledged.

Something in her died. He hadn't come to reunite, or to let her patch the problem she'd created. He was—

"Leaving New York," he said as if tuning into her despair.

Confused, she blinked. Then the words righted. "You *are*?"

He set the suitcase in the snow, came the last distance of the snowbound path. Slowly, he climbed the stairs, halting on the step below. Her gaze leveled with that resolute and stubbled chin.

Snowflakes dappled his hair, his big shoulders, clung

to his eyelashes. "Dad's coming along to help with the personal stuff. I wanted to come here first. I've sold my condo, Ella. Quit NHC."

"I know," she whispered. "Peter told me last night. He told me…. Oh, J.D. Can you ever forgive me?" *Please touch me. Please hold me.* Her eyes smarted.

"Nothing to forgive, honey." And then he brushed away the tear that spilled to her cheek. "I should've told you right off about my decisions, but I wanted it to be done with, to come back here free and clear of anything unsavory."

"And then I made a mess of it condemning you with—"

"Shh." He touched her lips gently with a finger. "That's done and over. We all take a left turn now and again." Smiling, he set his forehead to hers, caught her hands in his. "I want to start again, Ella."

"Me, too. Where will you live?"

He raised his head. "Well," he said with a wry grin. "Considering Dad brews the best damned espresso north of New York and creates a clam chowder that would make Bostonians cry, and considering those are my two favorite food groups, I don't think I have a choice here."

She laughed. "Your stomach's chosen well."

"So has my heart," he said, the grin slipping. "I love you, Ella. I've never said that to a woman, nor do I intend to say it to another. You fill me to overflowing. I want to make a family with you—if you'll take a chance on a briefly unemployed business geek."

Laughing through a mist of tears, Ella wrapped her arms around his neck. "Yes," she said, crazy for his scent, the one mixed with snow and the day's beginnings and wonder. "Every chance. I love you, J.D. I thought I'd lost you and I didn't know how to get you back. Oh, God." She began to cry in earnest.

"Ah, babe. You had me from the get-go. All you did was look into my eyes with that ophthalmoscope and I was a goner."

She cupped his cheeks. "There's an administrator's job coming open in two months…"

"I know. Peter got me an application."

"We Wilders know a good man when we see one."

"And what do you see?" he whispered.

"The man I want to sleep beside for the next fifty years."

"Only fifty?"

"Okay, sixty."

"Make it seventy and it's a done deal."

She smiled into his summer eyes where their future lay and then he kissed her. And it was long and wonderful and warm and told her of his heart and, when he lifted his head, she nodded to the suitcase in the snow. "Why don't you bring that inside for a minute?"

His grin was powerful. "Think I will."

He kissed her again, and the snow fell in hushed beauty around them.

* * * * *

*Mills & Boon® Special Edition brings you a
sneak preview of Cathy Gillen Thacker's*
The Gentleman Rancher,
which is available in March 2009.

*When Taylor O'Quinn left Texas to pursue a
writing career, Jeremy Carrigan missed his former
best friend more than she'd ever know. Seeing
her again makes him want more than just the
camaraderie they used to share. Can he convince
the now-famous novelist to help a certain doctor
turned gentleman rancher stay put in Laramie – as
Jeremy's friend, lover and wife?*

*Don't miss this exciting new story coming next
month in Mills & Boon® Special Edition!*

The Gentleman Rancher

by

Cathy Gillen Thacker

Trouble In Paradise?

Newlyweds Zak and Zoe Townsend may act like love-birds on their reality TV show, detailing the most intimate moments of their first two years as husband and wife, but on the set of their first feature film, *Sail Away*, the mood has been anything but romantic. The pop/rock stars have been at each other's throats since filming began two months ago. Why, no one seems to know, least of all the legions of fans who have rooted for the Hollywood couple since their fairytale romance began…

June 1 edition, *Celebrities Weekly* magazine

As the sun went down, bringing dusk to the West Texas sky, Taylor O'Quinn had been in her Jeep Liberty for seventeen hours and fifty-three minutes. By her calculations, she had about twenty more minutes to go before arriving at the Chamberlain ranch, outside of Laramie, Texas. She couldn't get there a moment too soon.

Her air-conditioning had begun malfunctioning somewhere near the California-Arizona border. By the time she reached

New Mexico, it had quit altogether. Driving with the windows down hadn't been so bad when she was up in the mountains, but when she had hit the flatlands of Texas, the heat had been brutal.

One-hundred-and-ten degree summer heat—even when blowing over her body at sixty-five miles an hour, was still hotter than blazes. The only thing keeping her going was the thought of the swimming pool awaiting her. Well, that and the fact that she had a place to stay rent-free for the next few weeks. Another fringe benefit was no one would ever think to look for her at the family home of her best friend.

Speaking of which… Taylor pulled over long enough to loop the hands-free receiver over her ear and dial her cell.

Paige Chamberlain answered on the third ring. "Hey, girl-friend, where are you?"

Her familiar voice brought a smile to Taylor's face. "About fifteen minutes away, I think."

"Great!" Paige exuded her customary good cheer and stellar organizational skills. "I left a key for you in the planter next to the door. Help yourself to anything in the fridge. The yellow guest room in the main house is yours. Clean towels are in the linen closet across from the hall bath." After a brief interruption, she returned to the line. "I've got an appendec-tomy to do, so I'll be at the hospital a few more hours. Until then, make yourself at home."

"I will. And thanks, Paige."

The sound of an announcement over the hospital intercom system blared in the background. "No problem." Paige shouted to be heard above it. "See you soon!"

Taylor said goodbye and concentrated on finding the un-assuming entrance to the ranch, a task that was not so easy as dusk covered the Texas countryside with a soft gray gloom. Luckily, the plain black wrought-iron archway, sans lettering of any kind, was just as Taylor remembered it. She turned down the single blacktop lane and drove through unkempt fields of mesquite and scrub brush that remained wild until she was completely out of sight of the two-lane farm-to-market road. Then, the fence started, the grass grew more manicured, and the sprawling hacienda-style ranch house rose above the plain, glowing with welcoming lights. The personal retreat was an oasis of privacy and rustic comfort, the kind of home where legendary actor-film director Beau Chamberlain and his movie-critic wife, Dani, could live in relative anonymity. Taylor had stayed there many times when she and Paige had been college—and med school—roommates.

Acutely aware of just how long ago that had been—a good seven plus years—Taylor parked in the empty driveway and got out. Leaving her belongings in the car, she passed the front of the house and followed the flagstone path to the backyard. The pool was designed to look like a hidden lagoon, complete with waterfall and tropical plants. The underwater lights weren't on, but there was enough illumination from the adjacent ranch house and the guesthouse on the opposite side to allow Taylor to take a swim.

The shimmering blue water beckoned, cool and inviting.

Deciding to heck with going back to search for her swimsuit—she had waited far too long for relief from the searing summer heat as it was—Taylor kicked off her sandals and reached for the hem of her sweat-sticky T-shirt. Suddenly a familiar masculine voice jolted her from the task at hand.

"I wouldn't, if I were you."

IT FIGURED, Jeremy Carrigan thought, that the first time he'd gone skinny-dipping in years, he'd get caught with his pants off. By none other than the most aggravating woman he had ever had the misfortune to meet in his life.

Taylor O'Quinn turned to get a closer look.

In profile, she'd been beautiful.

Facing him, she was even lovelier. In the years since he'd seen her, the delicate bone structure of her facial features had only become more pronounced. Long-lashed blue eyes dominated a slender nose and full, soft lips. As she released her thick black hair from the elastic band that had been holding it away from her face, the windswept strands fell rippling across her slender shoulders and brushing at the graceful slope of her neck. Lower still the perfection continued in her five-foot-six form. His pulse picked up as his glance roved her full breasts, slender waist, curvy hips and long, shapely legs.

Somehow, Jeremy thought, it wasn't all that surprising to find that Taylor O'Quinn had only gotten sexier as she aged. What stunned him was the realization that, even after all these years of resentful silence, he still wanted her as much as ever.

Taylor froze—as if sensing she were being scrutinized. Slowly, she peered into the shadowy cove where he was lounging. When she spied him, her chin took on the familiar tilt. "What are you doing here?" Taylor demanded.

Jeremy put up a staying hand to keep her from coming any closer. "I might ask the same question of you," he remarked dryly, silently wishing his response to her would fade.

"Paige said I could stay here with her for a few weeks while her own house is being remodeled and her parents are in Montana. She didn't say anything about you being here."

Jeremy shrugged. "She didn't tell me anything about you arriving, either."

Still a good twenty-five feet away from him, Taylor knelt to test the temperature of the water with her hand. "Then you're just here to swim?" She regarded him with lifted brows.

The way she'd said that told Jeremy she wasn't here just to get in a workout, either. Which probably meant Paige had